The Butterfly Club

www.**randomhousechildrens**.co.uk

HAVE YOU READ THEM ALL?

WHERE TO START

THE DINOSAUR'S PACKED LUNCH
THE MONSTER STORY-TELLER

FOR YOUNGER READERS

BURIED ALIVE!
CLIFFHANGER
GLUBBSLYME
LIZZIE ZIPMOUTH
SLEEPOVERS
THE CAT MUMMY
THE MUM-MINDER
THE WORRY WEBSITE

FIRST CLASS FRIENDS

BAD GIRLS
BEST FRIENDS
SECRETS
VICKY ANGEL

HISTORICAL ADVENTURES

OPAL PLUMSTEAD
QUEENIE
THE LOTTIE PROJECT

ALL ABOUT JACQUELINE WILSON

JACKY DAYDREAM
MY SECRET DIARY

FAMILY DRAMAS

CANDYFLOSS
CLEAN BREAK
COOKIE
FOUR CHILDREN AND IT
LILY ALONE
LITTLE DARLINGS
LOLA ROSE
MIDNIGHT
THE BED AND BREAKFAST STAR
THE ILLUSTRATED MUM
THE LONGEST WHALE SONG
THE SUITCASE KID

MOST POPULAR CHARACTERS

HETTY FEATHER
SAPPHIRE BATTERSEA
EMERALD STAR
DIAMOND
THE STORY OF TRACY BEAKER
THE DARE GAME
STARRING TRACY BEAKER

STORIES ABOUT SISTERS

DOUBLE ACT
THE BUTTERFLY CLUB
THE DIAMOND GIRLS
THE WORST THING
ABOUT MY SISTER

FOR OLDER READERS

DUSTBIN BABY
GIRLS IN LOVE
GIRLS IN TEARS
GIRLS OUT LATE
GIRLS UNDER PRESSURE
KISS
LOVE LESSONS
MY SISTER JODIE

ALSO AVAILABLE

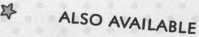

PAWS AND WHISKERS
THE JACQUELINE WILSON
CHRISTMAS CRACKER
THE JACQUELINE WILSON TREASURY

☆ ABOUT THE AUTHOR ☆

Jacqueline Wilson is one of Britain's bestselling authors, with more than 35 million books sold in the UK alone. She has been honoured with many prizes for her work, including the Guardian Children's Fiction Award and the Children's Book of the Year. Jacqueline is a former Children's Laureate, a professor of children's literature, and in 2008 she was appointed a Dame for services to children's literacy.

Visit Jacqueline's fantastic website at
www.jacquelinewilson.co.uk

Jacqueline Wilson

The Butterfly Club

Illustrated by Nick Sharratt

DOUBLEDAY

THE BUTTERFLY CLUB
A DOUBLEDAY BOOK 978 0 857 53317 3
TRADE PAPERBACK 978 0 857 53318 0

Published in Great Britain by Doubleday,
an imprint of Random House Children's Publishers UK
A Penguin Random House Company

This edition published 2015

1 3 5 7 9 10 8 6 4 2

Text copyright © Jacqueline Wilson, 2015
Illustrations copyright © Nick Sharratt, 2015

Penguin Random House is committed to a sustainable future for our business, our readers
and our planet. This book is made from Forest Stewardship Council® certified paper.

Set in New Century Schoolbook

Random House Children's Publishers UK,
61–63 Uxbridge Road, London W5 5SA

www.**randomhousechildrens**.co.uk
www.**totallyrandombooks**.co.uk
www.**randomhouse**.co.uk

Addresses for companies within The Random House Group Limited
can be found at: www.**randomhouse**.co.uk/offices.htm

THE RANDOM HOUSE GROUP Limited Reg. No. 954009

A CIP catalogue record for this book is available from the British Library.

Printed and bound in Great Britain by Clays Ltd, St Ives plc

To Tilly and Harry

And in memory of Lily Rose

Chapter One

There are three of us. Phil and Maddie and me.

We all have fair hair cut in fringes. I once tried to cut mine myself. Whoops!

We have blue eyes, and Dad says we have button noses. He sometimes pretends to pinch them but it doesn't hurt.

Phil's proper name is Philippa. I sometimes forget how you spell it and get the 'l's and 'p's muddled up.

Maddie's proper name is Madeleine. Her name's hard to spell too. I put the 'e's and 'i's in the wrong place.

My name's Tina. It's easy-peasy to spell, thank goodness.

We are triplets. *Surprise!* Everyone thinks I'm the little sister. It's very annoying. I was the littlest even when we were born. I was very, very little.

I didn't grow big enough when we were all inside our mum. I think Phil and Maddie must have sat on me and squashed me. When we were born I was too little to go home with Mum and Phil and Maddie. I had to stay all by myself in a tiny metal cot with a lid on it called an incubator. Well, I expect I had my teddy. I couldn't wear proper baby clothes, and I had to wear a silly little hat to keep my head warm.

The doctors found out that I had something wrong with my heart. Perhaps it was too small, like me. I had to have an operation. They put a tiny little box in my chest to make my heart pump properly. Thank goodness they put me to sleep so I didn't know anything about it.

I nearly died. I did, truly. I'm not meant to know but I've heard the grown-ups whispering about it. Mum and Dad came to visit me every day, while Gran and Grandad looked after Phil and Maddie. Mum cried because she couldn't give me a proper cuddle. I had to stay inside my incubator.

But I got better! I was even allowed out into the open air!

I grew nearly big enough to go home, but then I got a chest infection and had to have lots of medicine. I didn't have it in a spoon like I do now – the nurse just dripped it straight into my arm. I'm sure she was very gentle. I like nurses. I still have to go to the hospital for check-ups and they always make a fuss of me.

Anyway, I got home at last. I could be with Phil and Maddie again. They were still much, much bigger than me.

They stayed bigger.

I was a bit scared when I started school because I was so much smaller than all the other children. I wasn't used to lots of big children. I'd never played their kind of games.

Mum was a bit scared too. She had a word with the Reception teacher, Miss Oxford.

'I'm worried about Tina because she's still very delicate. She's got a w-e-a-k h-e-a-r-t and can't take too much rough and tumble. Phil and Maddie know they have to be gentle with their sister, but perhaps the other children won't understand. Do you think you could keep a special eye on Tina?' she said. She spelled out weak heart, but I knew what she was talking about even though I couldn't read yet.

Miss Oxford was very kind.

'Of course, Mrs Maynard. Don't worry. How lovely to have triplets in my class! You all look very special girls. Would you like to sit together?'

'Yes please!' we said.

Miss Oxford watched over me in the playground whenever she could.

Phil and Maddie looked after me too. If the big boys played chase and barged into me, my sisters got very angry. If the girls – like horrible Selma Johnson – wouldn't let me join in their games, then Phil and Maddie shouted at them.

Oh goodness, that Selma! I hated her. She was the biggest girl in the class with a great red scary face. Her hair was pulled back in such a tight ponytail it made her look even scarier, especially when she pulled a silly face. She was boss of the whole class, even the boys. She pushed and she poked and she called people mean names. She couldn't even be bothered to work out the difference between Phil and Maddie. It's easy, even though they are very, very alike.

Look closer!

Phil has a tiny mole on her cheek. She doesn't like it, but Gran says it's her beauty spot. Maddie has a scar on her chin from when she fell over the first time she tried to skateboard. She's absolutely brilliant at skateboarding now. Phil gets annoyed because Maddie is better than her. I don't know if she's better than me because I'm not allowed to do skateboarding.

mole

scar

Maddie's always the best at sporty things, especially football. She jokes about a lot but she's very brave. She always stands up for Phil and me. Phil is the sensible one. The teachers always pick her to run errands. She's top of the class. She nearly always gets ten out of ten and a gold star. Maddie gets at least nine out of ten. I'm not going to tell you what *I* get. Sometimes Phil and Maddie help me.

Selma calls both Phil and Maddie Dim Twin – which is very stupid, because Phil and Maddie aren't dim at all, they're very clever. It's especially stupid because they're not twins, they're triplets.

Selma calls *me* Little Bug. This is even more insulting, though actually I quite like bugs.

I don't mind worms. I can pick them up. It's great fun, because Phil and Maddie run away screaming. I'm good with spiders too. Do you know something – even Mum is scared of spiders! And I like caterpillars, with all their little feet. They tickle when they go for a walk up your arm. I particularly like ladybirds because they're so pretty. I've got a red dress with black spots and

I call it my ladybird dress. Phil has a pink dress with white spots and Maddie has a blue dress with yellow spots. I like mine best. We wear our spotty dresses to parties.

We just go to little parties. There's a funny boy called Harry in our class, and when we were in Year Two he invited us all to a football birthday party. Phil and Maddie and I wanted to go — especially Maddie, because she loves football.

'I'm sorry, chickies, it's out of the question,' said Mum. 'You know Tina isn't allowed to play rough games like football.'

'Why can't Phil and I play?' asked Maddie. 'Tina could watch us. You wouldn't mind, would you, Tina?'

I would have minded a little bit, because it's rubbish not being able to join in, but I shook my head.

'Maybe I could go to the football party too,' said Dad. 'I could kick a ball about with Tina on the sidelines while the other kids play. Then she can have a bit of fun too.'

We all thought this a great idea, but Mum still

said no. It's because she worries about me. She can't help it.

So we couldn't go to Harry's party. It was a great shame, because I like Harry a lot. One time we had to clear up the paints together and we got a bit carried away. I painted him a black moustache and he painted me great red lips so that we looked like two grown-ups. I painted Harry with red on his nose because lots of old men have red noses – my grandad does. Harry thought I might like to dye my hair like a big lady and so he started painting it black.

Miss Evelyn, our Year Two teacher, hardly ever got cross, but she went a bit berserk when she saw Harry and me. We had to be washed very thoroughly.

Then Phil and Maddie and I had *our* seventh birthday. Mum and Dad gave us *our own iPad*!

We thought this very cool and grown up, though we wished we had one each. We've got used to sharing and taking turns, but it's very boring having to wait for the iPad. Especially for me, because I nearly always have to wait till last.

Mum and Dad *did* give us new flowery satchels for when we started in the Juniors. Mine didn't hold quite as much as Phil's and Maddie's, but Mum said a proper big one would be a bit too heavy for me.

Gran gave us three Victorian dolls with frilly dresses. This was a weird present because we were getting a bit big for dolls, weren't we? Though we still liked to play games with our Monster High dolls.

We couldn't play games with our Victorian birthday dolls because they were too precious. They just had to sit on our windowsill like ornaments. It was hard to pretend they were real, but we did give them names.

'I'll call mine Rosa, because she's carrying a bunch of roses,' said Phil.

'I can't call mine Hankie!' said Maddie.

'Perhaps you could call her Sneezy, like that little man in *Snow White*?' I suggested.

'Why don't you call your doll Primrose, Maddie, because she's got a pale yellow dress. And then you can call your doll Rosebud, Tina, because she's a bit smaller than ours. There – they've all got three lovely matching rosy names,' said Phil.

We told Gran what we were going to call our dolls and she was very pleased.

I thought Rosebud was a bit boring, but I liked her little baby. I took off her tiny dress. She wasn't wearing any knickers! I gave her a red swimming costume with my felt tip and took her for a swim in the bath.

Baby's scarlet swimming costume faded away

but she didn't mind swimming naked. I had to keep hold of her or she sank. *I* didn't mind. Dad has to keep hold of me when we all go swimming or else *I* sink.

Baby liked playing all sorts of games. She flew, she climbed the curtains, she parachuted off the top of the wardrobe, she explored the great dark cave of the fireplace. She even braved ferocious wild beasts. They're not *really* wild beasts, they're our new birthday hamsters! Grandad gave us some money and we decided we all wanted to buy a pet. So we went to Pets at Home with him.

'I want the brown one in the corner, chomping away on all the food! I shall call him Nibbles,' said Phil.

'I'll have that fawn one racing round and round. I'll call him Speedy,' said Maddie.

'I'll have the really, really big yellowy one right there,' I said, pointing. 'He'll be the boss of the other two and help them do everything. I shall call him Cheesepuff.'

We decided we really, really liked being seven.

Chapter Two

We had a wonderful time that summer. We went to the seaside for two whole weeks! We'd only been on holiday for a week before. We didn't always go away.

Phil and Maddie and I sometimes went to stay with Gran and Grandad in the school holidays.

But *this* summer Mum and Dad and Phil and Maddie and I went on a fortnight's holiday to Norfolk! We stayed in a caravan. There were lots and lots and lots of caravans, like a special caravan village.

As we were there for two whole weeks, Nibbles and Speedy and Cheesepuff had to pack their tiny bags and go to stay with Gran and Grandad.

We sent them a postcard.

Dear Gran and Grandad and Nibbles and Speedy and Cheesepuff
We are having a lovely time. Gran, please don't feed Nibbles too much as he's very greedy and can sometimes be sick. Especially don't feed him chocolates. Love Philippa

We have races on the beach and I always win! We go swimming every day. We even went in yesterday when it was ~~raining~~ raining. Love Madeleine

Mr and Mrs B. Maynard
42 Melrose Gardens
Wardle
Bishopsgrave
B1 2GT

I love love love it here.
Love Tina ×××

I really *did* love it in the caravan. It was a bit of a squash when we were all inside, especially when we went to bed, though that just made it more fun. We were mostly outside, even for meals. I helped with the cooking! Well, Mum didn't want me to have a turn frying the sausages as she said I was too small and they kept spitting fat – but I *did* cook baked beans one day, and everyone said they were delicious.

We ate heaps and heaps on holiday. And we had an ice cream every single day! Mum fussed that she was putting on weight. By the end of the fortnight she couldn't get her shorts zipped up properly! I hoped I might put on weight too. And grow a bit. I kept measuring myself against Phil and Maddie. I didn't seem to be having much luck.

We took our teddies on holiday because they didn't mind being packed flat in a suitcase. (You obviously can't do that with hamsters.) The first day we took the teddies paddling, but that was rather a disaster. They got very wet and had to spend a long time on the washing line.

Mum got a bit cross. 'Really, girls, you should

have had more sense! You can't take teddy bears swimming!'

'It was meant to be just paddling, Mum, but they got excited and splashed a bit,' said Phil.

'Splashed rather a lot,' said Maddie.

'I think *my* teddy might have splashed the most,' I admitted guiltily.

'They were just having a bit of fun,' said Dad.

'But they're their special teddies – the ones they've had ever since they were born,' said Mum. 'I think you'd better keep them in the caravan when they've dried out.'

So the teddies had to have an indoor holiday

after that. I think they felt a bit fed up, though we left them little treats to eat.

I took my Baby out with me every day. She had a *lovely* time. She came swimming with me and it didn't hurt her at all.

We made her a special sandcastle. Dad did a lot of the hard digging. Phil and Maddie made a moat and filled it with sea-water. Mum found shells and seaweed, and *I* did the decoration. Then I put Baby on top of her castle and Dad took a photo of her. Baby loved being on top because she's so little – though she's very, very brave. She didn't even flinch when a great flying dinosaur attacked her.

We didn't want to go home. We wanted to stay on holiday for ever.

'I wish we could stay here on holiday too, girls,' said Dad, 'but we've all got to go back to work.'

Dad works in a supermarket. He has special clothes for work.

18

Mum works part time in a building society. She has special clothes for work too.

I suppose Phil and Maddie and I go to work as well. We work at school. We had to have special new clothes for the Juniors. We'd always worn red sweatshirts in the Infants. But we're not infants any more. We wear green sweatshirts now.

I crayoned a green sweatshirt on Baby so she could come to the Juniors with me.

'My goodness, don't you all look grown-up girls,' Mum said on the first day of term.

'Our big girls, in the Juniors!' said Dad.

'It's going to be scary being in Miss Lovejoy's class!' said Phil.

Miss Lovejoy was famous for being very, very strict. She had such a soft, pretty name, but she wasn't soft and she wasn't pretty. We all knew about Miss Lovejoy, even in the Infants.

And now she was going to be our teacher for the whole of Year Three!

'I'm not scared of Miss Lovejoy,' said Maddie. 'I'm going to love being in Year Three. We'll be playing netball and football!'

'Yes, I need to have a word with Miss Lovejoy,' said Mum. 'I don't want Tina playing games.'

'Poor Tina,' said Maddie.

'I don't mind.' I decided I'd play games with Baby instead.

'Finish up your cereal then, girls. We don't want to be late on your first day in the Juniors!' said Mum.

We had to rush around cleaning our teeth and going to the loo and putting on our sweatshirts and our new outdoor shoes.

Baby is very lucky. She hasn't got any teeth to clean. She never needs to do a wee. She doesn't wear school uniforms and shoes.

Dad kissed us all goodbye and wished us luck. I held Baby up so she could get a kiss too.

'Oh my goodness, why has she gone green?' asked Mum.

'That's her school uniform,' I said.

'No, Tina. You can't take her to school. She'd only get lost or broken. And you're not allowed to take toys to school in the Juniors.'

'Baby isn't a toy, she's a person.'

'She's a person to you, but to everyone else she's a little china doll. Put her back with your big doll – and when you get home you'd better give her a good scrub,' said Mum.

'But I'll be so lonely without her!' I whimpered.

'Of course you won't be lonely. You have Phil and Maddie to keep you company,' Mum told me.

'I want Phil and Maddie *and* Baby,' I wailed. I opened my eyes wide so that they'd water. I was very good at making myself cry. It nearly always made Mum and Dad pick me up and give me a cuddle and let me have my own way. It *always* worked with Gran and Grandad.

But today Mum was a bit snappy.

'Come on, Tina, we haven't got time for an

argument. You don't want to make us all late for your first day in the Juniors, do you?'

I saw that crying wasn't going to get me anywhere, so I ran upstairs with Baby. But I didn't put her back with big Rosebud. I tucked her away in my school skirt pocket.

Then we set off with Mum. It felt very grown-up to be walking right past the Infants' entrance, all the way to the Juniors.

'I'm going to come in with you, girls,' said Mum.

'Oh, Mum. People will think we're babies,' said Maddie.

'Mum's not fussed about us, silly. It's Tina,' said Phil.

'She needn't be fussed about me. I'm not a baby. I'm exactly the same age as you,' I said.

But secretly I was quite glad that Mum was coming through the Juniors' gate with us. It felt a bit strange being in the Juniors' play-ground. The Juniors were very big. Some of them were practically grown-up. They stared at us – they stared at me in particular. I edged in between Phil and Maddie. I wanted to hold their hands but I didn't want to look even more of a baby.

'Let's find this Miss Lovejoy,' said Mum, marching into the school building.

'Mum! I don't think we're allowed inside yet!' said Phil.

'We're supposed to stay in the playground until they ring the bell!' said Maddie.

'I know, but I'm sure Miss Lovejoy won't mind,' said Mum.

23

Miss Lovejoy looked as if she minded a lot when we found our new classroom.

'Ah . . . school hasn't quite started yet,' she told us.

'Yes, I know, but I wanted to have a little word with you about my girls.' Mum spoke in the firm voice she always uses when she's giving us a telling-off. But Miss Lovejoy's voice was much, much firmer.

'Your triplets, Philippa and Madeleine and Tina?' she said. She obviously knew the register by heart already.

'That's right. Phil and Maddie are identical, as you can see – though if you look carefully, Phil has a mole on her cheek and Maddie has a little scar on her chin.'

'I dare say I shall learn to tell them apart,' said Miss Lovejoy.

'And then there's Tina.' Mum took hold of me and gave my shoulders a little squeeze. 'I don't know whether you've been told about Tina . . . As you can see, she's got a bit of catching up to do. She was very ill when she was born. She had to have major heart surgery and she's had various problems since. She's not allowed to play any contact sports, and I'd appreciate it if you kept an eye on her in the playground.'

Miss Lovejoy looked at me. I didn't *want* her to keep an eye on me. It was too fierce and beady.

'Don't worry, Mrs Maynard,' she said. 'I'm sure Tina will flourish in my class.'

I didn't think I was going to flourish. I thought I might very well wilt.

'Off you pop now, girls,' Miss Lovejoy went on, extra firmly.

It was clear that she expected Mum to pop off too. So we all did as we were told.

'Well,' said Mum, when we were out in the playground again. 'She's a bit of an old dragon, isn't she?'

'Yes!' said Phil.

'Yes!' said Maddie.

'Yes yes yes,' I said.

'But I dare say she's perfectly lovely when you get to know her,' Mum added quickly.

We weren't sure we really *wanted* to get to know her.

Chapter Three

When the bell rang for the start of school, Phil and Maddie and I ran fast so we could be first in line. Then we marched very, very quickly in through the door and down the corridor to our classroom.

It wasn't because we were eager to start lessons with Miss Lovejoy. We just needed to get to the classroom first so we could get a good seat. Maddie forged ahead when we were inside and bagged three places at the table right at the back. Selma Johnson tried to push her out of the way, but Maddie was very fierce and brave. She got her bottom on one seat. Phil shoved her way onto the other. I squeezed in between them. There! We had the perfect seats, and there was nothing Selma could do about it. She couldn't just tip us off, not with Miss Lovejoy's beady eyes on us.

Some of the boys wanted to be on our table too.

'No, go away, this is a girls' table,' said Phil.

'Yes, push off. Go and find your own table,' said Maddie.

So they went away to sit at another table at the side. I was a bit disappointed. One of the boys was Harry. I'd have liked to have him on our table.

But some quite nice girls, Sophie and Neera and Carys, came and sat with us. We all smiled at each other.

'There!' said Maddie proudly. 'I got us the perfect table.'

Everyone else barged about the room until they found places too. All this time Miss Lovejoy was standing by the whiteboard watching us, arms folded. Her eyes were extra beady.

'Have we finished playing Musical Chairs?' she

said eventually. She didn't shout, but she used the sort of voice that makes you sit up straight and quiver.

'Welcome to Year Three. I am your teacher, Miss Lovejoy. I hope you will learn many things while you are in my class. We're going to start learning straight away. You might have pushed and shoved and run wild in the Infants, but now that you are in the Juniors it's time you learned some manners! Now stand up!'

We stood up.

'Pick up your school bags and line up by the door!'

We did as we were told. We thought she was mad as we'd only just sat down, but no one dared argue, not even Selma Johnson.

'That's better,' said Miss Lovejoy. 'Now, you will sit where *I* tell you. Is that understood?'

We all nodded.

Miss Lovejoy's beady eyes looked up and down our line. She started picking children at random and pointing to tables. She mixed girls with boys. She put Selma Johnson right at the front!

Then she pointed to Phil and told her to go to

a table at the side. Phil went to sit down. Maddie followed her, pulling me along too.

'Excuse me,' said Miss Lovejoy. 'Where are you going, Madeleine?'

She was the first teacher we'd had who could tell the difference between Phil and Maddie.

'I'm going to sit with my sister, Miss Lovejoy,' said Maddie. 'And so is Tina.'

'Did I *tell* you to sit with Philippa?'

'No, but we always sit together. We have ever since we were in Reception.' Maddie was very red in the face.

'We don't want to be a nuisance, Miss Lovejoy, but Maddie and I have to look after Tina,' Phil said quickly.

'I believe *I* am the teacher,' said Miss Lovejoy. 'It's *my* job to look after all of you. Now, go and sit at the table on the other side of the room, Madeleine. Quickly! And you, Tina, come and sit here.'

Oh no! She pointed at the table at the front. She actually pulled out the chair next to terrible Selma Johnson.

'Sit here!' she said.

I clutched Baby tight in my hand for courage. 'Mum says I have to sit with my sisters,' I said in a tiny voice.

Miss Lovejoy cupped her hand behind her ear. 'I beg your pardon?' she said.

I didn't dare repeat it. I sat down next to Selma. She moved her chair away as far as

31

she could, pulling a face.
I tried very hard not to
cry. One tear escaped – and
Selma saw.

'Cry-baby!' she hissed.

Then Miss Lovejoy
said that Kayleigh had to
sit at our table. Selma smirked. Kayleigh wasn't
mean when Selma wasn't around, but when she
was with Selma she could be really horrid. She
gave really painful Chinese burns.

So I had Selma on one side and Kayleigh on
the other!

I hoped that some of the quite nice girls would
be sent to join us. But the other three were boys –
two big rough boys, Peter and Mick, and Alistair
Davey. Alistair was quite small (though nowhere
near as small as me), but even so, he had a very
loud voice. He always knew the answers to all
the questions. He spoke in an extremely know-it-
all way, even to the teachers.

If we had to have a boy at our table, I wished
it could have been Harry.

So there we were. Selma, Kayleigh, Peter, Mick, Alistair and me. The worst table ever. I craned my neck round to see Phil. She shook her head at me in sympathy, looking terribly worried. I peered round at Maddie. She pulled a sad face at me.

I slid further and further down my chair, feeling smaller than ever. Perhaps I could turn into a little girl-mouse and scamper across the floor and out of the door.

'Everyone settle down. Now, I need someone sensible to give out these lovely new exercise books,' said Miss Lovejoy. Her beady eyes swivelled around the room.

Phil sat up straight. She was nearly always picked to be book monitor. And flower monitor and cloakroom monitor. In the Infants she was famous for being reliable.

But this was Miss Lovejoy's class in the Juniors.

'You, Selma! Come and give out the exercise books, please,' she said.

Oh no! Was *Selma Johnson* going to be

teacher's pet? I was doomed, doomed, doomed.
I sank down further.

'Sit up properly, Tina!' said Miss Lovejoy.

I wriggled upwards, staring at the table
because I didn't want to look at anyone.

'And put your head up! Goodness me, you're
slumped like a little old lady!'

Mick and Peter chuckled.

Phil put up her hand.

'Yes, Philippa?'

'Excuse me, Miss Lovejoy, but
I don't think Tina is feeling very
well. I think she'd feel better if she
could sit next to me. Or Maddie.
She isn't used to being on her own,'
said Phil, very bravely indeed.

'She isn't on her own, Philippa. She's sitting
with five other children. Now stop worrying
about your sister. She's perfectly all right. Aren't
you, Tina?'

No, I wasn't perfectly all right. I felt very, very,
very wrong, but I didn't say anything. I sat as
still and silent as Baby.

Miss Lovejoy raised her eyebrows. I wondered if she was going to shout at me. Or smack me. Perhaps she had a cane in her cupboard and was going to beat me . . .

Grandad had told us what school was like when he was a little boy. The teachers always shouted or threw chalk at you or whacked your hands with a ruler, and if you were very naughty you got the cane. Six times, on your bottom!

35

Grandad said teachers weren't allowed to punish children like that nowadays. But Miss Lovejoy was very old. Perhaps she was still stuck in the old days.

She didn't shout or smack or fetch a swishy cane from the cupboard though. She just shook her head at me.

'Now, children, I want you to write on the top line of your new exercise books: *My Summer Holidays.* I shall write it out on the board for you, because you don't want to start your brand-new book with a spelling mistake, do you? What do you think I want you to write about?' she asked.

We stared at her. Was this a trick question?

'Come along, wake up!'

Phil put her hand up. 'You want us to write down what we did during our summer holidays?' she said, a little nervously.

'Brilliant deduction, Philippa,' said Miss Lovejoy. 'Right, get started, everyone. I want at least two pages. And while you're writing, I want each of you to come out to me in turn. I want to hear you reading.'

There was a big sigh all around the room. Two whole pages! And how terrifying, having to read out loud, standing beside Miss Lovejoy.

It was my turn first!

I felt my throat go dry when Miss Lovejoy pointed and beckoned. I had to stand really close to her. She smelled of peppermints and washing powder. She had a lot more wrinkles when you got near her.

'Start reading, Tina,' she said.

I swallowed. I opened my mouth. No sound came out. I clutched Baby, who was hidden in my left hand.

'Come on, Tina.' Miss Lovejoy pointed to the first word. 'What does this say?'

She had short, stubby, very clean nails. My gran has long pointy red nails. Mum has short nails, but sometimes she goes to a nail parlour and then she gets amazing nails, even longer than Gran's, with pretty sparkly patterns on them. Phil and Maddie and I can't wait until we're old enough to go to a nail parlour.

'Tina, I'm waiting. Now, I know you can read. Off you go,' said Miss Lovejoy.

I knew I could read too. But I prefer being read to. Phil and Maddie sometimes pretend I'm their little girl and they take turns reading me stories.

Mum reads to all three of us. She reads us stories she liked when she was a little girl.

Dad reads to us out of his old comic books. He does all the funny accents and acts it out.

Gran reads to us from her magazines. She tells us all about famous people.

Grandad doesn't read to us from a book or a comic or a magazine. He tells us stories straight out of his head.

He always starts in the same way: *Once upon a time there were three sisters with hair the colour of honey and eyes as blue as the sky.* We chant the words along with him.

Grandad's stories might start in exactly the same way, but then each one becomes entirely different and brand-new. There's a story about the three sisters taming a wild lion and a ferocious bear and a stampeding elephant. There's a story about the three sisters flying to the moon in a space rocket. There's a story about the three sisters growing fish tails and swimming the seven seas. There's a story about the three sisters climbing the highest mountain in the world and setting up home with two yetis and their yeti cubs. There's a story about the three sisters in a Victorian orphanage getting the better of a wicked matron. There's a story about the three sisters capturing wicked pirates and finding an amazing treasure chest. There's a story about the three sisters going back to the time of the dinosaurs and meeting up with a Tyrannosaurus Rex. Oh, there are so many stories.

'*Tina!*' said Miss Lovejoy. 'Stop daydreaming and *read*.'

She frightened me. I wasn't used to grown-ups shouting at me, and I felt my eyes go all teary again. I looked at the page, but the words were swimming up and down like little fish.

Then, suddenly, there was a rush and a jostle on either side of me. Phil was on my left side, Maddie on my right.

'Please, Miss Lovejoy, we always read together,' said Phil.

'Tina can't do it on her own, but she can when we're with her,' added Maddie.

'Can we just show you how we do it, please, Miss Lovejoy?' asked Phil.

'Please please please, Miss Lovejoy?' said Maddie.

'Philippa! Madeleine! Are *you* the teachers in this classroom?' said Miss Lovejoy.

'No, but we're Tina's sisters, Miss Lovejoy.'

'And we're just bursting to show you that Tina can read nearly as well as us.'

'Well, I don't want you bursting in my classroom because I'm the person who would have to clear up the mess,' said Miss Lovejoy. 'Very well. Read together. Just the first paragraph, to get Tina started.'

We all stared at her, amazed. Had we actually got the better of Miss Lovejoy?

She handed us the book. We all held it, me squashed in between my sisters, and Phil started reading.

'*Once upon a time there was a fiddler who travelled far and wide, playing his music wherever he went,*' she read.

'*Folk laughed and clapped whenever he played,*' Maddie read.

Then they both nudged me. I took a deep breath. I stared at the next sentence. I rubbed my eyes. The words stopped swimming up and down.

'*Little children used to sing along with the music. They clapped their hands in time to the tune. Sometimes they danced. The fiddler spread happiness wherever he went,*' I read.

I mastered every word. I read all the way down to the bottom of the page. I managed to put expression into it too, so that it sounded like a real story.

Phil smiled at me. Maddie smiled at me. Even Miss Lovejoy smiled at me!

'There!' she said. 'Well, now I know you can read so well, Tina, I shall expect you to do it all by yourself next time. Sit down now, girls.'

I worried about *next time* – but at least the ordeal was over for today! I sat down next to Selma, my knees still a bit wobbly. She pulled a hideous face at me. So did Kayleigh. I tried to pull one back, but I don't think it was very scary.

It was Selma's turn to read to Miss Lovejoy next. I couldn't help hearing. She didn't read very well at all. She kept stumbling over words and mixing up her 'were's and 'where's, and she couldn't work out how to pronounce the word *magician*. It was a big surprise.

She looked fiercer than ever when she sat back down. 'What are you staring at, Little Bug?' she hissed.

'I'm not staring at anything,' I said. 'I can't

help my eyes looking at you because you're right bang next to me.'

'I wish I wasn't! I hate and detest having to sit next to a dim little cry-baby like you,' said Selma.

'I think *you're* the dim one,' I said. Unwisely.

Selma dug her sharp elbow right into my ribs and then kicked me hard on the ankle under the table. I couldn't help giving a little squeal of pain.

Miss Lovejoy heard, even though Alistair was booming confidently in her ear, reading as if he were on a platform addressing the whole school.

'Hey, hey, Tina, Selma! What are you two up to? How dare you scuffle about in my classroom! Settle down at once and get on with your holiday writing,' said Miss Lovejoy. She'd stopped smiling now. She'd gone back to being mean and scary. We knew we'd better get on with our work – or else!

I opened up my new exercise book. I selected a newly sharpened pencil from my pencil case. I licked the lead a little to make it come out nice and black. I was all set, but I couldn't get started.

I wasn't used to writing my own stories. Phil and Maddie and I made up lots of stories together. Sometimes they started like Grandad's Three Sisters stories. Sometimes they were stories we made up all by ourselves.

Phil liked to make up family stories. She invented great big families with lots of children. She drew them all and gave them special names.

Maddie liked to make up adventure stories.

Her favourite was a story about children going up in a special balloon and landing in all sorts of different countries.

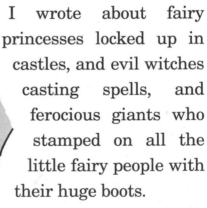

I liked to make up magic fairy-tale stories.

I wrote about fairy princesses locked up in castles, and evil witches casting spells, and ferocious giants who stamped on all the little fairy people with their huge boots.

I loved drawing all my fairy-tale people, but I didn't write down the stories myself. My hand couldn't keep up with the story inside my head and I forgot how you spelled the words. So I just said it out loud, and Phil or Maddie scribbled it down for me.

If we were sitting together at the table, then they'd help me, the way they'd always done in the Infants. But now I was on my own. It was horrible.

I knew we were supposed to write two pages, but by the end of the lesson I'd only managed this:

We did lots in the sumer holadays. We went to the beech. We did swiming. We mad a cassel.

Chapter Four

Miss Lovejoy wasn't impressed by my story. She didn't think much of my multiplication either. She got cross when we started our Ancient Egyptian project because I muddled up my 'g's and 'y's and 'p's, even though she wrote the title out on the board for us.

I had to squeeze Baby tightly to stop myself crying. I knew how Selma would scoff at me. But after a bit I started to get interested in the Ancient Egyptians. Especially the mummies. Even the ordinary people looked interesting in Ancient Egyptian pictures. They all walked sideways in those days – even their dogs and their cats and their gods!

At break time Phil and Maddie and I played at being Ancient Egyptians.

Oh, it was so lovely being with my sisters! They were very kind and comforting, and felt soooooo sorry for me because I had to sit next to Selma Johnson.

'We'll tell Mum,' said Phil.

'Yes, she'll come and tell old Lovejoy that we've *got* to sit together,' added Maddie.

At least we could sit together at lunch time. We have our own lunch boxes with cats on, but mine's red, Phil has pink and Maddie has blue.

We had *exactly* the same for lunch. We had a cheese sandwich with two tiny tomatoes and a carrot stick. Then we had an apricot slice. Last of all we had a shiny red apple, with orange juice to wash it all down.

Phil and Maddie ate all theirs up. I got a bit full and bored of eating so I left some of mine.

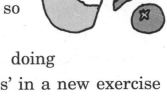

It didn't matter. Phil and Maddie ate it up for me, so Mum wouldn't get cross.

After lunch we started doing something called 'Life Cycles' in a new exercise book. We began with caterpillars.

'Excuse me, Miss Lovejoy, but we've already learned all about them in the Infants,' Alistair boomed.

'Thank you so much for informing me, Alistair,' said Miss Lovejoy. 'However, I'm about to refresh your minds and remind you all over again about the wonder of metamorphosis. Who knows what that long word means?'

Alistair knew, of course.

'It's when caterpillars spin a cocoon and later emerge as butterflies. It's brilliant!' he shouted.

'Indeed,' said Miss Lovejoy. 'Right, everyone, look at the caterpillars on your worksheet. Copy one very carefully.'

We'd painted caterpillars in the Infants, but we were allowed to do any old green blobs. In Miss Lovejoy's class we had to do it properly, putting in every segment, with the little feet in the right places. We could use our coloured felt tips. We didn't have to stick with green.

I very carefully copied a black-and-white-striped caterpillar with a red head. Well, it might have been its red bottom – it was difficult to tell.

Selma's caterpillar looked a mess. She'd tried to do a spiky caterpillar, but she drew the spikes in such a hurry that they just looked like scribble.

'Oh dear, Selma, I think you'd better turn over your page and start again,' said Miss Lovejoy.

She tutted when she saw Kayleigh's cater-pillar too. 'Kayleigh, you haven't looked properly. Caterpillars don't have feet on every single segment.'

'Mine's not a caterpillar, it's a centipede,' said Kayleigh.

'Did I *tell* you to draw a centipede?' asked Miss Lovejoy. 'No, I did not!'

She looked at Peter's caterpillar. She had to look really hard because it was so small, not much bigger than an eyelash. 'My goodness, Peter, you're going to have to draw bigger than that. I'm an old lady. You'll have to consider my eyesight,' she said, squinting.

She couldn't miss Mick's caterpillar. He'd drawn a huge one, with great fangs and horns and claws.

'Mine's not a mini-beast. It's a great big monster-beast, miss,' he said proudly.

'Miss *Lovejoy*. Well, it's certainly monstrous, Michael. Top marks for imagination and bottom marks for biological accuracy.'

'You what, miss— Miss Lovejoy?'

'Miss Lovejoy means that you've done it all wrong, and you have to do it one hundred per cent right when you do biology. Biology means the study of all living things,' Alistair said importantly.

'What are you – a walking Wikipedia?' said Mick, and everyone sniggered.

Even Miss Lovejoy's lips twitched, though she frowned at him.

'Well done, Alistair,' she said when she looked at his caterpillar. 'You will be pleased to know that it's absolutely one hundred per cent biologically accurate.'

Then she looked at my stripy caterpillar. 'Well done, Tina!' she said. 'Very well done. My goodness, you're excellent at art. Your stripy caterpillar is absolutely splendid.'

She smiled at me and I smiled back, forgetting to be scared. Down on the page my stripy caterpillar smiled too, delighted to be admired.

Then Miss Lovejoy moved on to the next table. 'Let's see this caterpillar then, Little Bug,' said

Selma. She snatched my exercise book. 'Hmm. I don't think it's very good at all, do you, Kayleigh?'

'I think it's totally rubbish,' Kayleigh agreed.

'What happens when caterpillars get tired of being caterpillars?' Selma gave me a painful nudge. 'Go on, Little Bug, what happens?'

I didn't want to answer her. I sat tight, clutching Baby under the desk.

'*I* know what happens – it's easy-peasy,' said Alistair. 'They turn into a chrysalis. They spin all this stuff so that it's like a duvet all round them.'

'You're absolutely right. One hundred per cent right,' said Selma. 'So let's give your caterpillar a chrysalis, Little Bug.' She took her black felt pen and scribbled hard all over my stripy caterpillar, even his little red head or bottom.

It felt as if she were scribbling all over me too.

54

There was a shocked silence at our table. Then Kayleigh laughed a little uncertainly.

The three boys stared.

'What did you go and do that for?' said Mick.

'Did you do that for a joke?' asked Peter.

'It looks a terrible mess now. Whatever will Miss Lovejoy say?' said Alistair.

They all looked at me.

'Are you going to tell on Selma, Tina?'

I *wanted* to tell. I so, so, so wanted Selma to get into trouble for destroying my beautiful caterpillar. You're always told to tell on someone if they've been mean or nasty. But people in our class don't like it if you go running to a teacher. You get called Telltale. And if I told tales on Selma, then she'd be even meaner and nastier to me, if that were possible.

I shook my head and closed my exercise book because I couldn't bear to look at Selma's scribble any more. I sank down low on my seat, clutching Baby so hard that she dug a hole in my hand.

Then, at long last, the bell went for the end of school.

'Right, everyone, put your exercise books in the book bag on the back of your chair. Good afternoon, Class Three,' said Miss Lovejoy. She looked at us. 'I expect you all to say *Good afternoon, Miss Lovejoy.*'

'Good aft-er-noon, Miss Love-joy,' we said.

'Off you go then,' she said, making little waving signs with her hands. She picked up her big bag and went out of the classroom.

Phil and Maddie came rushing up to me.

'What's the matter, Tina?'

'Did Selma do something?'

I couldn't say anything. I just opened the page of my book so that they could see the scribble.

'Oh, Tina! And Miss Lovejoy said it was a very good drawing – I heard her,' said Phil.

'So Selma scribbled all over your drawing? Well, let's scribble all over hers!' said Maddie.

'No, Maddie!' said Phil. 'Then we'll be just as hateful as Selma. Look, I know what we'll do, Tina. Watch!'

She took my exercise book and very carefully tore out the scribbled page – and the page it was joined to at the back.

'There! Put the book in your satchel and then you can do another lovely caterpillar at home. How about that?' suggested Phil. 'That's a good idea, isn't it, Tina?'

I gave a little nod.

'I still think it's a better idea to muck up all Selma's things.' Maddie took Selma's exercise book out of the book bag on the back of her chair and picked up a felt tip.

'Maddie! Don't you dare!' said Phil.

Maddie put them back reluctantly. Maddie is the noisiest of us, but somehow Phil is the boss.

'Come on then. Mum will be waiting,' said Phil.

We ran out of the classroom, down the corridor and across the playground. There was Mum, waving at us. We all waved back like anything and then ran over to her. We had a big, big, big hug.

'Hello, my lovely grown-up girlies. How did you get on?' she asked.

'Oh, Mum, Miss Lovejoy's so mean! She won't let us sit together!' said Maddie.

'I asked her ever so nicely and tried to explain that we have to look after Tina, but she wouldn't listen!' said Phil.

I opened my mouth to say something too – but instead I burst into tears.

'See, Mum! See how upset Tina is! It's because she has to sit in between the two worst girls in the class. Kayleigh and *Selma Johnson*!'

'Selma!' said Mum, sounding shocked. Selma was famous for being hateful. Even the mums knew about her. The only mum who liked Selma was Selma's own mum, and even *she* didn't always seem to like her very much.

'Yes, and Selma scribbled all over Tina's caterpillar!' said Phil.

'I wanted to scribble all over Selma's caterpillar but Phil wouldn't let me,' said Maddie.

'Quite right too,' said Mum. 'Oh dear, oh dear. Poor little Tina.'

She picked me up and gave me my own individual hug. Phil and Maddie are too big for proper up-in-the-air hugs, but I'm still little enough.

'There now. Let's get you home,' said Mum.

She carried me part of the way, but I started to get a bit too heavy even though I'm little. So she carried my satchel instead, and Phil and Maddie took turns carrying my lunch box.

When we got home Mum made us strawberry smoothies and gave us each a gingerbread man. No – it was a gingerbread *girl* with a skirt and yellow icing on her head like hair. They were all identical.

'Triplets,' said Phil.

'Like us,' added Maddie.

'No, wait a minute,' I said. I'd cheered up a lot now and I was hungry because I hadn't eaten all my lunch. I nibbled my gingerbread girl's skirt until half of it was gone. '*Now* they're like us!'

'There now,' said Mum. 'Tell me all about school. Are you girls sitting at entirely different tables then?'

'Yes, and it's horrid without Maddie and Tina,' said Phil. 'Though actually I'm quite lucky, because I'm sitting next to Neera and she's got lovely long plaits. Mum, do you think we could all grow our hair and have plaits too?'

'I don't really fancy tackling three pairs of plaits every morning!' said Mum. 'Are you sitting next to a nice girl, Maddie?'

'I'm sitting next to a boy! I'm quite lucky because it's Harry and he's ever so funny,' said Maddie.

'Well, I'm ever so unlucky,' I said. 'I'm sitting next to Selma, and she's the worst girl in the world.'

I was glad for Phil because I knew that Neera was a very nice girl. I'd have liked to sit next to her myself if I couldn't be with my sisters.

I was glad for Maddie because I knew that Harry was a very nice boy. I'd have *especially* liked to sit next to him myself if I couldn't be with my sisters.

I drooped against Mum and she gave me another cuddle.

'Don't worry, Teeny Weeny,' she said. This was my special private baby name. 'I'll go and see Miss Lovejoy tomorrow. I'm sure she'll let you girls sit together when I explain.'

But she didn't sound very certain.

When Dad came home from work he wanted to know all about our first day in the Juniors. So we told him.

Then Gran and Grandad Skyped, and they wanted to hear all about our first day too. We had to act it out for them.

Then we went up to our bedroom. Phil and Maddie played while I spent half an hour redrawing my caterpillar. I tried even harder this time.

We were very, very tired by bedtime. We didn't

whisper much when Mum put the light out. We all went to sleep. But I had funny dreams all night long. I dreamed that I was a caterpillar and Selma was going *stamp, stamp, stamp* on me.

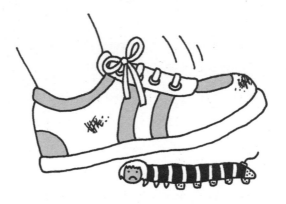

Chapter Five

The next morning Mum came into school with us again. Miss Lovejoy was in the classroom looking busy, busy, busy.

'Ah, Mrs Maynard. Again,' she said.

'I'd like to have a little word with you about my girls, Miss Lovejoy.' Mum's voice was very steady but her hand had gone damp. I knew because I was holding it.

'That would be lovely,' said Miss Lovejoy, in a voice that clearly said, *No it wouldn't.* 'However, I'm a bit tied up preparing for the morning's lessons. I'm generally around after school to have a chat with parents. Perhaps you'd like to catch me then.'

'Yes, but I just wanted to ask you if the girls can sit together today. I believe you've seen for yourself that they really need to be together, especially when it comes to reading. It gives Tina so much more confidence if she can be with her sisters,' Mum said bravely.

'I dare say,' replied Miss Lovejoy. 'But she's not going to be with her sisters for the rest of her life, is she? I think it's about time Tina learned to stand on her own two feet. It will be good for Philippa and Madeleine to make some new friends too.'

'Yes, but surely it's a bit soon, especially for Tina.'

'I think it's high time, *especially* for Tina,' said Miss Lovejoy. 'Now, I really must get on with my work.'

Mum still didn't give up. 'Then if the girls really can't sit together, I wonder if Tina could move to another table.' She lowered her voice. 'She's a bit frightened of Selma. I'm sure she's a lovely girl, but she can be rather . . . intimidating.'

I hadn't heard that word before, but I knew what it meant.

'I understand your concern, Mrs Maynard,' said Miss Lovejoy. 'But Tina has to learn to get along with everyone and to fight her own battles. We can't keep her wrapped up in cotton wool for ever.'

Mum went pink. Dad sometimes says that too. Mum *would* like to keep me wrapped up in cotton wool.

Maybe bubble wrap would be better! Then I could give it a little pop every now and then when I was bored.

'I did try to make it clear that Tina's rather delicate, Miss Lovejoy.' Mum's voice was almost as scary as Miss Lovejoy's now.

Phil and Maddie and I stared at our mum and our teacher. They were getting really angry. Oh goodness, what if they had a fight?

'I appreciate that Tina's health might still be delicate, but I rather think you're underestimating her,' said Miss Lovejoy. 'Now, Mrs Maynard, I wouldn't dream of advising you on how to treat your daughters at home. I'm sure you don't want to advise me on how to deal with the children in my class at school.'

At that moment the bell rang.

'Oh my goodness, there's the bell!' said Miss Lovejoy. 'Now, if you'll excuse me, I must go and fetch the register. Good morning.'

'The old witch!' Mum whispered. 'Maybe I'll go and have a word with your head teacher.'

'Oh, Mum, don't! It wouldn't

be any use. I think even Mrs Brownlow is scared of Miss Lovejoy,' said Phil.

'Oh, Mum, better not say anything or we'll get into trouble big-time,' said Maddie.

'Oh, Mum!' I said. I couldn't manage any more.

'My poor, poor, poor girls!' Mum tried to give us a quick hug, but children had started coming into the classroom. Maddie and Phil wriggled away, embarrassed. I stayed where I was. I needed all the hugs I could get!

Then Mum had to go and we started the second day of school. It was worse than the first. Well, some of the lessons were quite interesting. We did some more about the life cycle of the butterfly and learned all about cocoons.

Selma stared and stared and stared when I opened my exercise book and she saw the beautiful black and white caterpillar with the red head (or bottom).

'What's happened to all the scribble, Little Bug?' she asked.

'Did you manage to rub it all off?' said Kayleigh.

Even the boys stared.

'How did you do that?' Selma nudged me again with her pointy elbow. 'Hey, I'm talking to you!'

'I magicked all your scribble away,' I said.

'What?'

'I just looked at the page and used my secret magic power and made the scribble vanish.'

'You never!' said Selma – but she looked as if she might believe me.

'OMG!' said Kayleigh. (Mum hates that expression. She won't let us say it. It sounds very grown-up.)

'Wow!' said Peter.

'Holy cow!' said Mick. (I don't think Mum would like that expression either.)

But Alistair spoiled it. He shook his head at the others. 'There's no such thing as magic,' he said.

'Yes there is, Brainbox. What about all them shows on the telly?' said Mick.

'They're just clever tricks,' said Alistair. 'And Tina's played a clever trick on you lot.'

'So how's she done it then, Sherlock Holmes?' asked Selma.

'Easy-peasy. She's torn out the scribbled-on page and done her caterpillar over again. Simple.'

I felt very annoyed with Alistair. I sooooo wanted everyone to think I had magic powers. Especially Selma.

After life cycles we had to do writing. Only Miss Lovejoy mixed up writing with life cycles, because she wrote on the whiteboard *A Day in the Life of a Caterpillar.*

'You what, miss?' asked Mick.

'Miss *Lovejoy*!' said Miss Lovejoy. 'And don't use that uncouth expression. Surely the meaning of the title is obvious. I want you all to write about a day in the life of a caterpillar.'

'Yes, but what caterpillar, miss— Miss Lovejoy?' said Peter.

'Any caterpillar. Make up a story about one.'

'Can it be a monster caterpillar, Miss Lovejoy?' said Mick.

'Yes, it can. This is a story so you can make up anything you want.'

'Can it be a story that is one hundred per cent true, Miss Lovejoy?' asked Alistair.

'Yes, it can. Now, get started, everyone. Copy down the title into your writing books. And pay strict attention to the spelling on the whiteboard!' said Miss Lovejoy.

I paid strict attention to the spelling – but not quite strict enough. I got my 'a's and 'e's a bit muddled. I looked at the board but didn't manage to write it the same way on the page.

A day in the life of a catarpiller

Miss Lovejoy came and checked and sighed deeply. 'Look, Tina, look! Dear me. I think you'd better write out caterpillar five times before you get started so that you can remember the correct spelling in future,' she said.

So I had to copy it out very slowly to make sure I got it right. While I was doing this, I started to make up my story in my head. I imagined being very, very, very small, a little black-and-white caterpillar with a red head (or bottom). I would have big problems hiding from birds. All the ordinary green caterpillars would just crawl into a bush or a tree and hide amongst the leaves, and the birds wouldn't have a clue where they were. I'd have to find a black-and-white hidey-hole.

Simple! I decided I'd make friends with a zebra. I was pretty sure zebras didn't eat caterpillars. So I trekked all the way to the zoo – a tremendously long trek if you're a very weeny caterpillar. I didn't have to pay because caterpillars go free. I saw yellow lions and grey elephants. There was a stripy tiger, but he was too orange. I saw black and white penguins, but they didn't have stripes. But *then* I saw a zebra. 'Hello, Mr Zebra,' I said in as loud a voice as I could manage. 'Hello, little Miss Caterpillar,' said the zebra. 'Would you care to jump up into my mane? I will carry you wherever you want so long as you give my head a little scratch whenever it gets itchy.' So I jumped up onto his mane and lived there very happily indeed, and every morning when the zebra woke up with an itchy head, I went *scratch, scratch, scratch* with my weeny feet and scratched all the itch away.

If Phil or Maddie had been next to me to write it all down, then it would have been a very good story. But they weren't there – I had to write it all myself, and my hand was already aching after copying the word *caterpillar*, and I didn't have much time left for my story.

It didn't come out right. Miss Lovejoy wasn't impressed.

I am a litel weeny caterpiller. I am scared of burds. I have a zebra frend.

At break time Phil and Maddie told me what they'd written. Phil wrote a story about a man caterpillar making friends with a lady caterpillar in a cabbage patch and them having lots of babies.

'Miss Lovejoy said it was nicely written and I got all my spellings right,' said Phil, 'but she pointed out that it wasn't very accurate because caterpillars don't mate. I thought that was mean – she said we could write anything because it was a story. And I made up lovely caterpillar babies called Christopher and Carol and Colin and Crystal.'

'I made up a story about a race between all the insects in the garden,' said Maddie. 'The caterpillar was nearly always last because its legs are so little, but then it drank some fertilizer and grew great enormous legs so it could dash along and beat everyone else. Miss Lovejoy said it was very imaginative, but she didn't like the fertilizer bit because she said it would be deadly poisonous. That was mean too, because fertilizer in stories doesn't *have* to be poisonous. It's not as if *I'm* going to drink fertilizer.'

'I made up a story about a weeny black-and-white caterpillar and a zebra. Miss Lovejoy didn't like the spelling and said that it wasn't long enough and I hadn't tried hard enough,' I said mournfully. 'I *hate* it in Miss Lovejoy's class.'

I thought I might like the next lesson because it was art and Miss Lovejoy had said that I was very good at art. But we didn't do any proper art in this art lesson. We did cutting out with scissors.

Miss Lovejoy told us about a man called Matisse who did cut-out pictures of snails and strange people and weird shapes. She hung copies of his cut-out pictures on the wall.

Then she got Selma to hand out coloured paper to each table – red and yellow and blue and ordinary white – and a pot of paste, and a pair of scissors each. They weren't *proper* scissors, they were silly baby ones without points. Still, perhaps this was just as well as I was sitting next to Selma.

We had to do our own cut-out pictures, sticking coloured shapes onto the white paper.

I wanted to draw my shapes first in case I went wrong.

'No, no, put that pencil away, Tina. The whole point is to free yourself up and make big bold shapes,' Miss Lovejoy told me.

I didn't like doing big bold things. I liked to draw everything, rubbing it out if it went wonky, and colouring it in very carefully, not going over the lines. I liked to *choose* my colours too. Red and yellow and blue were a bit limiting.

I had a picture in my head. I knew exactly what I wanted it to look like.

But when I tried cutting it out, it went all wrong. 'That's rubbish!' said Selma.

She was right – it *was* rubbish. Phil's head was too small, and poor Maddie lost one of her legs

75

when the scissors wobbled, and I was lopsided, as if I were falling over. The colours were wrong too. We looked as if we'd been using Gran's hair-dye and had a bad case of sunburn.

'*My* picture's much better!' said Selma.

She was right again. She hadn't tried to make anything up, she'd simply copied Matisse and stuck blobs of paper in a snail shape. But it worked.

It was very, very annoying.

'Well done, Selma! That's exactly what I wanted,' said Miss Lovejoy.

Selma smirked all over her face.

At the end of the lesson Phil and Maddie came to look at my cut-out. I could see that they were all prepared to admire it. They looked for a while without saying anything.

'Well, it's quite good,' said Phil, meaning, *It's very, very bad.*

'Did that horrible Selma nudge you when you were cutting out?' asked Maddie. 'I bet she did. She jogged you so you chopped off my leg and a chunk of Phil's head.'

'Of course!' said Phil. 'And I bet she nudged you again when you were sticking and that's why you're all lopsided, Tina.'

Now this hadn't happened at all. I didn't *say* it did.

'I don't want to tell tales,' I said instead. It wasn't exactly a lie.

Then I put my chin on my chest and looked sad. So of course Phil and Maddie thought that Selma really *had* nudged me and made me spoil my cut-out picture. It wasn't really my fault – was it?

They were positively fuming. They said all sorts

of bad things about Selma. It was very enjoyable.

Then they went storming up to her at lunch time. I tried to stop them – I didn't want my sisters to get hurt because Selma can be horrid. But I didn't want them to find out the truth either. It was no use. They got to Selma long before I could catch up with them.

'Just you leave my sister alone!' said Phil.

Selma looked up, very surprised. 'What you on about? I didn't do anything!'

'You mucked up Tina's cutting out!' said Phil.

'I did *not*!' said Selma. 'Now clear off or I'll thump you one.'

'You're a wicked liar. And don't threaten us, or *we'll* thump *you*,' said Maddie.

She shoved herself right up to Selma to show that she wasn't a bit scared (though she was). She shoved a little bit too hard. She bumped into the table and her hand caught Selma's open lunch box. It went flying off the edge, and Selma's crisps and Coke spilled everywhere.

It was an accident, but Selma thought she'd done it on purpose.

'You little whatsit!' she said – but she didn't say *whatsit* at all. She said a much worse word. Mum would faint if she heard any of us use that word.

Selma stood up, her fists clenched. Maddie took a step back. So did Phil. I took *several* steps back. Selma looked ready to bash all three of us.

But then one of the dinner ladies came charging over.

'Now then, what's all this, girls! Oh dear, look at this mess all over my clean floor! For goodness' sake, why do you have to be so clumsy?' she said to Selma.

'It wasn't my fault, miss! It was that triplet! She did it on purpose!' cried Selma.

She pointed. She pointed at *Phil* – which was plain stupid, because Phil would never threaten to thump anyone or accidentally-on-purpose knock their lunch box over.

Selma was stupid to muddle us up. It's as plain as anything: Phil has the little mole, Maddie has the scar on her chin.

The dinner lady was glaring at Phil. 'Is that true? Did you knock her lunch box over?' she asked.

'No, it's not true at all!' Phil looked upset and indignant and totally, totally telling the truth. Which she was.

'Then you're a naughty girl to try to blame someone else,' the dinner lady said to Selma. 'Now pick up those bits while I get a cloth for all that spilled Coke.'

Selma started to protest furiously.

'You be quiet, young lady, or I'll report you to your teacher,' said the dinner lady. 'You're in Miss Lovejoy's class, aren't you? What will *she* say if I tell her you've spilled your lunch, blamed an innocent friend, and bad-mouthed me into the bargain!'

That shut Selma up. We went to sit at the other end of the canteen. We had to keep out of Selma's way now. She hadn't liked us before, but now we were deadly enemies. And I still had to sit next to her in class!

Chapter Six

'I'll get my own back on you!' Selma hissed.

And she did. Terribly. Day after day.

She poked me with her elbows. She kicked me under the table. She pulled my hair. She broke my pencil. She opened my lunch box and bit into my fruit bar, and then spat it out again because she said she didn't like it. She flipped my special rubber in the shape of a teddy bear over to the other side of the classroom and I never found it again.

 She sellotaped a note to my back saying *Kick me!* She pulled up my skirt in the playground so that everyone could see my knickers. She threw

the ball right at my head when I was sitting watching our class play dodgeball.

I didn't have Phil and Maddie nearby to look after me, so I had to take Baby to school, day after day. Mum noticed she was missing once, when she was tidying our room.

She was very cross. 'Tina, I've *told* you not to take that baby doll to school! You'll only break her or lose her. She's not a toy, she's an ornament. Gran paid a fortune for those dolls. Now, promise me you'll leave her on the windowsill with Rosebud,' said Mum.

'Yes, Mum, I promise,' I said.

I couldn't keep my promise. I needed Baby with me sooooo much. I *had* to take her to school every single day, but I always kept her completely hidden.

I was very good at it. I could tuck her up in my hand and you couldn't see her, not even her neat little china feet. If I needed both hands free, I put Baby in my skirt pocket. She liked it in there. I put a tissue inside so she had something soft to curl up in, and a few biscuit crumbs in case she was hungry. She was very good. She never tried to peep out or wriggle free.

Nobody knew she was there. Well, Phil and Maddie did, but they're my sisters. Nobody *else* knew. Even Miss Lovejoy with her beady eyes didn't know that Baby came to school every day. Selma didn't have a clue about Baby. Until one dreadful day . . .

We were doing life cycles again. Our caterpillars had made their cocoons and then magically emerged as butterflies. We had to draw a British butterfly, copying from a book.

Selma did a large white so that she could just draw it on the white page, putting in two dots on each wing, and then say she was finished.

Kayleigh thought this was a good idea and copied her.

Peter did a small white. It was so weeny you could hardly see it.

Mick did an elephant hawk-moth. He coloured it carefully in pink and brown, but then added a trunk and tusks.

Alistair did a small tortoiseshell. He spent ages trying to get the orange and black markings one hundred per cent right. He got very cross when the wings didn't quite match.

I decided to do a peacock butterfly because I like red. I drew the four false eyes on its wings very carefully in black and light brown and blue, edged its wings with dark brown, and gave it long distinctive antennae.

I don't want to sound as if I'm boasting, but it was a truly splendid picture. Miss Lovejoy circled our table, looking to see what we'd done. She tutted at Selma and Kayleigh, saying they hadn't tried very hard. She told Peter she'd have to start bringing a magnifying glass to school. She shook her head at Mick and told him to rub out the trunk and the tusks. She said Alistair had tried very hard. But when she saw my butterfly she clapped her hands.

'What a wonderful peacock butterfly, Tina!' she said. 'Look, everyone!' She held it up so that the whole class could see. Phil and Maddie looked so proud of me. Selma was scowling and scowling. I suddenly stopped being happy and started to get very scared. She had scribbled all over my black-and-white stripy caterpillar with the red head (or bottom). What would she do to my beautiful peacock butterfly?

But she didn't do anything to my peacock butterfly. She couldn't.

'I think your drawing is so exceptional it deserves a gold star, Tina,' said Miss Lovejoy.

The whole class gasped. Some teachers give you gold stars at the drop of a hat. In Miss Oxford's class in the Infants you got a gold star just for writing your own name. *I* got one – though I have got a very easy name. But Miss Lovejoy was famous for never ever giving gold stars. You were lucky if you were given a measly tick, even if you got ten out of ten.

'Do you know what I'm going to do?' said Miss Lovejoy. 'I'm going to very, very carefully tear your butterfly out of your school book and pin it up on the wall because it's so special. Then I can look at it when I want cheering up. You can *all* look at it. You'll see what you can achieve if you try hard. Are you listening, Selma and Kayleigh?'

Kayleigh looked upset. Selma scowled some more. She seemed to be scowling with her whole body now.

'But then Tina won't have a butterfly in her life cycles book, Miss Lovejoy,' said Phil.

'Tina can draw and colour a brand-new butterfly while the rest of you are having a dodgeball lesson,' said Miss Lovejoy. 'I wonder if you've ever had to re-draw anything before, Tina?'

I gave a wriggle that could be yes and could be no. I was pretty sure that Miss Lovejoy knew all about me magicking away the scribbled black-and-white caterpillar with the red head (or bottom). Miss Lovejoy seemed a bit magic herself, the way she always knew about things.

She eased my peacock butterfly out of my exercise book and put it in a picture frame. The picture frame had glass, so Selma couldn't scribble over it, even if she'd dared.

I had a very peaceful time drawing a new peacock butterfly while everyone else played dodgeball. For once I didn't mind that I wasn't allowed to play exciting games because I was small and a bit poorly. I kept well out of the way of the balls so that Selma couldn't thump me with one.

I felt very happy. At lunch time, for the first time ever, I ate all my sandwich and all my crisps and all my fruit bar, and drank all my juice. I drank from the water fountain too. I pretended that I was a thirsty dog going *lap, lap, lap* and made Phil and Maddie laugh.

I wasn't used to drinking so much. I was very small. My bladder was very small too. Halfway through afternoon school I realized that I'd forgotten to go to the loo at lunch time. I hoped I'd be able to wait until the end of the lesson.

I got a bit fidgety. I felt all hot and squirmy. I started to worry I wouldn't be able to wait.

I didn't quite dare put up my hand and ask Miss Lovejoy if I could be excused. She was always very irritated and gave you great long lectures about going to the toilet at the right time.

The moment the bell went I absolutely charged to the girls' toilets. I didn't wait for Phil. I didn't wait for Maddie. I got to the loo *just* in time.

It was an enormous relief. I was washing my hands when someone came into the toilets. That someone was Selma. She was still scowling.

I stopped washing my hands. I flapped them wildly to get them dry and then made a dash for it. I didn't dash quite fast enough. Selma caught hold of me.

'You think you're absolutely it, don't you, you squirmy Little Bug,' she said. 'Teacher's pet!'

'I'm not!' I said.

'You are so. I'm well sick of you. I'm going to get you!'

I wasn't quick enough. She gave me an enormous shove that sent me flying. Baby went flying too, right out of my pocket. She skittered across the floor, way past the sinks.

'Baby!' I gasped, terrified that she'd break.

Selma ran fast. She bent down and grabbed Baby. 'What's this then?' she asked, peering at poor Baby. 'Oh, it's a little dolly-wolly. Still play with dolls, do you, Little Bug?'

'She's not a doll, she's an ornament,' I said. 'And watch out, she's china – she breaks very, very easily. Now give her back!'

I tried to snatch Baby, but Selma held her up high, miles out of my reach.

'Oh, little diddums wants her dolly-wolly,' she said, sneering at me. 'Well, you're not going to get her! She's mine now.'

'No she's not! She's *mine*! My gran gave her to me! Give her *back*!' I wailed.

'I don't really want this silly little doll. I think I'll just throw her away,' said Selma, taking aim.

'No, don't!' I screamed.

Selma could throw far and make balls bounce really hard. If she did that to Baby, she really would shatter.

91

'You can't stop me!' she said, laughing.

'Phil! Maddie!' I shouted at the top of my voice.

'Your precious sisters aren't here, are they?' said Selma. 'It's just you and me and funny little dolly.'

'Please don't throw her!' I begged, starting to cry.

'Oh, little diddums cry-baby! All right, I won't throw her.'

'You won't?' I said, snivelling.

'No, I won't. I'll flush her down the toilet instead!'

Selma ran into a toilet, slammed the door shut, and then I heard the chain being pulled.

'No no no!' I screamed.

'Yes yes yes!' said Selma, coming out of the toilet, grinning.

'You didn't!' I cried.

'Oh yes, I did!'

I rushed into the toilet and stared, hoping to see poor Baby bobbing up and down in the water. But there was no sign of her. Unless . . .

'You've just hidden her!' I said, running out again.

'Oh yeah?' said Selma. 'Where?' She opened both hands. She pulled out her pockets. She opened up her satchel and shook out the contents. She unzipped her pencil case. No Baby anywhere!

I threw myself down on the cold floor of the girls' toilets and howled. 'I'll tell!' I wailed.

'Tell all you like. I don't care,' said Selma, and she sauntered off, still smiling.

I stayed where I was, crying. Then I heard hurried footsteps.

'Tina!' It was Maddie.

'Oh, Tina, what's wrong?' gasped Phil, running after her.

'We've been looking for you everywhere,' said Maddie.

'What's happened?' Phil squatted down on the floor and put her arm round me.

'Is it that Selma?' asked Maddie, sitting beside me too. 'Has she hurt you? We saw her in the corridor and she had this weird smile on her face.'

'She did the most terrible thing ever,' I sobbed. 'She flushed Baby down the toilet!'

'She didn't! Are you sure? Even Selma couldn't be that hateful!' said Phil.

'She did, she did, she did!' I wailed.

'Which toilet?' said Maddie. 'I'll see if I can rescue her!'

'Oh, Maddie, don't, you'll get all germy,' said Phil.

But brave Maddie risked everything and stuck her hand right down the toilet. 'She's not there. She must have been flushed away and down the pipes,' she said, emerging with a dripping hand.

'Wash your hands! Wash them again and again! And then, when we get home, scrub them even more and dab some Dettol on them,' said Phil. 'And you'd better wash your face, Tina, it's all snivelly. Oh dear, Mum will be starting to worry, wondering where we are.'

'Wait till Mum hears what Selma's done!' said Maddie, washing fiercely.

'We can't tell Mum,' I cried. 'She told and told

me not to take Baby to school. I'll get in so much trouble if I tell.'

Maddie and Phil pondered.

'Yes, I think Mum would be very cross. Perhaps we could tell Miss Lovejoy . . .' Phil suggested uncertainly.

'She'd be cross too,' said Maddie. 'Look how narked she got when Harry brought his football game to school. She confiscated it for a whole week.'

'Well, she can't confiscate Baby because she's been flushed away,' said Phil.

I started howling all over again, thinking about poor Baby swimming in the sewers.

'Ssh now, Tina. Come on,' said Phil, washing my face for me. 'You'd better wash your hands one more time, Maddie. Wash right up your arms and under your nails too.'

'I've washed so much they're getting sore!' Maddie complained.

When we ran out across the playground at last, Mum was looking *really* worried.

'Why are you so late, girls? Everyone else came out a good ten minutes ago.' She looked at me.

'Oh, Tina, you've been crying!'

'No she hasn't, Mum. She's just had her face washed, that's all,' Phil said quickly.

'Yes, we've all been washing. Look at my hands!' said Maddie.

'How did you get them so dirty?' asked Mum.

'We . . . did painting at school. So we got all painty,' said Phil.

Mum looked at us all very closely. Her eyes were almost as beady as Miss Lovejoy's. 'Something's happened,' she said. 'Did you get into trouble with Miss Lovejoy today?'

'No, Mum!' we said in unison.

'Then was it Selma again? Is she still picking on you, Tina?'

I was still a bit too sobby to risk speaking, but I nodded my head.

'Poor Teeny Weeny,' said Mum, picking me up. 'Never mind. It's Saturday tomorrow and you're going out with Gran and Grandad. You can forget all about school and Selma for a little while. But then, on Monday, I'll have to have another word with Miss Lovejoy. Oh dear!'

Chapter Seven

I was soooo worried that Gran would want to see our dolls on Saturday. Mum hadn't yet noticed that Baby was missing, but Gran might. Rosebud's lap looked very empty.

'I know what we'll do,' said Phil. 'I'll take one of Rosa's roses and put it in Rosebud's hand. Yes – this little one that *looks* like a rosebud. Then it will look as if that's what she was holding all the time. Gran will forget that she used to hold a little china baby.'

'She might not forget,' I said.

'Well, tell you what, let's put Nibbles and

Speedy and Cheesepuff right in front of the dolls,' said Maddie. 'They won't mind us moving their cage. They'd probably like a change of view. And you know how weird Gran is about hamsters. She won't come anywhere near them, so she won't be close enough to look at the dolls.'

'Good plan, Maddie!' said Phil.

So we carefully moved the hamsters' cage over to the window, propping it up on top of our old doll's house.

'There!' said Maddie triumphantly.

'Brilliant!' said Phil.

'*Squeak, squeak, squeak* – we like our slight change of address!' said Nibbles and Speedy and Cheesepuff.

'But Mum will still notice,' I pointed out.

'Well . . . not yet,' said Phil.

'And she'll be very cross,' I added.

'Then you'll just have to cry lots, and she'll pick you up and give you a cuddle and stop being cross,' said Maddie. 'You know how to do it. You're the World Champion at stopping people being cross.'

'I'll say!' said Phil. 'So cheer up, Tina.'

I tried hard, but I couldn't quite manage it. I missed Baby so. Every time I thought of her my eyes went prickly and I couldn't swallow properly.

Gran and Grandad arrived and had a cup of coffee with Mum. (Poor Dad has to work at the supermarket most Saturdays.) We had to act as waitresses. Phil carried the tray of coffee because she has the steadiest hands. Maddie carried our juices, because her hands are almost as steady. I carried the plate of biscuits.

Then Gran went up to the bathroom and Phil and Maddie and I held our breath. Gran often pokes about when she's upstairs. After she came out of the bathroom we heard her going along the landing. Oh dear, she was heading for our bedroom!

We waited. We heard a little squeal. Had she spotted that Baby was missing?

'Why do you let the girls have those horrible little rodents in their pretty bedroom?' asked Gran, coming back into the living room. 'I'm sure it can't be very hygienic. And they *smell*!'

Oh, clever, clever Maddie!

Gran and Mum had a bit of an argument about the hamsters. We were all on Mum's side. Nibbles and Speedy and Cheesepuff *don't* smell. Well, only a tiny bit. Gran smells *lots*. She wears so much perfume it makes your nose itch, especially when she hugs you close.

But then Grandad made everyone laugh doing his hamster imitation, and Gran and Mum stopped getting at each other. We set off in Gran and Grandad's car while Mum said she'd catch up on the housework.

It's usually fun going in the car with Gran and Grandad. We sing all kinds of songs, we do hand dancing, we eat fruit drops, we play I Spy and Spot the Car, and we listen to stories. But today I didn't really feel like joining in. I was missing Baby too much.

'What's up with my little Teeny Weeny then?' asked Grandad.

'Nothing's up,' said Phil.

'You're fine, aren't you, Tina?' said Maddie.

I nodded. 'I'm OK,' I said in a very small voice. I wasn't very convincing.

'Is it school, pet?' said Gran. 'Your mum tells me there's some nasty girl – Sarah, Celia . . . whatever – who keeps teasing you. Is that right?'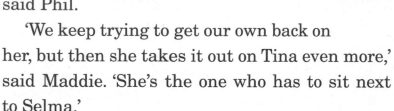

'She's called Selma, Gran, and she's absolutely horrible to our Tina,' said Phil.

'We keep trying to get our own back on her, but then she takes it out on Tina even more,' said Maddie. 'She's the one who has to sit next to Selma.'

'Well, why don't you ask your teacher if she can swap places?' asked Grandad.

'As if Miss Lovejoy would ever say yes!' said Phil. 'You could ask her ever so nicely . . .'

'You could go down on your knees and beg . . .' said Maddie.

'You could give her a huge bunch of roses . . .' said Phil.

'You could give her an enormous box of chocolates . . .' said Maddie.

'But she'd never, ever, ever say yes,' said Phil and Maddie together.

'Well, I think your mum should go in and tell her that it's simply not good enough,' said Gran. 'Poor little Tina!'

'Mum's going to see Miss Lovejoy again on Monday,' said Phil.

'But it won't be any use,' said Maddie.

'Well, don't let's get in a fuss about it now,' said Grandad. 'This is our day out, girls.'

'And first of all we're going shopping!' Gran told us.

We parked in a big shopping centre. Gran took us to our favourite shop and bought us each a little treat.

Phil chose very pale pink lipstick and nail varnish. Maddie chose a little  blue wallet. I couldn't choose for ages.

There was a lovely little bead purse that would have made a perfect bed for Baby – only I didn't have Baby any more.

There was a white feather boa that would have made Baby a wonderful wedding dress with a long train – only I didn't have Baby any more.

There was a little glittery ring that would have made Baby a beautiful crown – only I didn't have Baby any more.

'Come on, Tina – what would you like, poppet?' asked Gran.

I dithered. 'I don't think I want anything, Gran,' I said.

'Oh yes you do!' said Maddie.

'We'll help you choose,' said Phil. 'Look – what about these pretty slides? There's a blue butterfly slide!'

'Perfect!' said Maddie. 'Gran, did you hear about the beautiful butterfly Tina drew at school?'

'Miss Lovejoy said it was sooooo brilliant she gave Tina a gold star and hung it up on the wall in a special frame,' said Phil.

'Really? Well, perhaps your Miss Lovejoy isn't quite as bad as I thought she was,' said Gran. 'Well done, Tina, darling. You're a clever girl.'

 I felt a little bit better then. I did choose the slide, and it looked pretty when Gran put it in my hair.

Then we did some Gran shopping. She likes shoes.

I thought Grandad looked a bit lonely, so I went to have a chat with him.

'Don't you like shopping, Grandad?' I asked.

'I think it's a bit boring,' he said, pulling me onto his knee.

'What do you like doing best then, Grandad?'

'Eating!' he said. 'Hurry up, ladies! I want my lunch!'

We had a delicious lunch in a big food court. We all chose our favourite things.

Grandad had an Indian curry with rice and a can of lager.

Gran had a salad and a mineral water. She said she was being a good girl and sticking to her diet. But when she'd finished them, she weakened and chose a big cream éclair and a cappuccino for afters.

Phil and Maddie and I all chose the same. We had chips with tomato sauce and then great big knickerbocker glorys. They sound rude, but they're really amazingly huge ice-cream sundaes with whipped cream and cherries.

They were so big that even Phil and Maddie couldn't quite finish theirs. But they were delicious.

'Yum, yum, yum!' said Maddie.

'Yes, extra yum,' said Phil. 'Though we're not really supposed to eat chips without anything else. We'd better not tell Mum.'

'We're not supposed to eat ginormous ice creams either,' said Maddie.

'Oh, fiddle,' exclaimed Gran. 'You had tomato sauce with your chips. Tomato! That's a vegetable. And ice cream's dairy, made from milk and cream. Lots of calcium to make your bones strong.'

'Then we'd better feed this little mite ten knickerbocker glorys on the trot. She's got arms and legs like matchsticks,' said Grandad, giving me a hug. My new butterfly slide grazed his cheek, but he didn't mind.

'Where are we going now, Grandad?' asked Phil.

'Let's go and see some animals!' he said.

'Oh, goody – are we going to Pets at Home where we got Speedy and Nibbles and Cheese-puff?' asked Maddie.

'Nope. I'm thinking of *bigger* animals,' Grandad told us.

'Oh, are we going to that big park where they have all the deer?' asked Phil.

'Nope,' said Grandad. 'I think we're going to . . . the zoo!'

We all cheered. All except Gran. She's weird – she doesn't really like animals much.

'Isn't it a bit chilly for the zoo?' she asked.

'The girls are all wrapped up. I'll give Tina my scarf to keep her extra warm,' said Grandad.

Gran sighed. 'All right. If we must,' she said. 'At least it's put a smile on Tina's face.'

Gran didn't look very smiley as we wandered around the zoo. She had to keep sitting down and rubbing her feet because her new boots were hurting her.

We liked the monkeys best. We stared at them for ages. One was very rude, which made us get the giggles. The little yellow squirrel monkeys were our favourites. Phil started giving them all names.

'Look – there's Sarah Squirrel Monkey and Susan Squirrel Monkey and Sammy Squirrel Monkey and Simon Squirrel Monkey and – and Selma Squirrel Monkey,' she said, pointing.

'That's not Selma Squirrel Monkey. She's too pretty. That's Saskia. I'll show you Selma,' said Maddie, running to the next cage. She pointed to a baboon with a very big bare bottom. '*That's* Selma!'

We got the giggles all over again. I giggled so much I nearly fell over.

'Now then, stop being silly, girls,' said Gran.

'It does them good to have a bit of a laugh,'

said Grandad. 'Especially little Tina. I'm so glad she's cheered up at last.'

I was even cheerier when we went into Tropical World. I liked seeing all the rainforest animals, especially the giant sloth.

Phil and Maddie and I pretended that we were all giant sloths (I was a baby one) and we all moved very s-l-o-w-l-y.

Gran went through some plastic curtains at the end of the room, looking for another seat. Then she came back and beckoned. 'Come and look!' she said.

She'd found butterflies. Lots and lots of butterflies, all around us. There were blue ones and red ones and green ones and yellow ones and pretty patterned ones. They flew around our heads and landed on the shrubs and bushes so that we could get up close and look at them. Oh, I *loved* the butterflies! One flew right round Grandad and landed on his head! Lucky, lucky Grandad.

There were little stands of fruit here and there, so that the butterflies could have a little snack when they got tired of flying. A notice said that

they all came from a very hot country in Africa. I imagined what it might be like to be a little caterpillar crawling around amazing tropical flowers in blazing sunshine, then to go into a chrysalis and eventually wake up in a cold grey country like England. No wonder the butterfly enclosure was so warm that I had to get Gran to hold my jacket for me.

There were pictures of all the different butterflies, with their names. Phil and Maddie and I all picked our favourites and then tried to spot them.

'I like the emerald swallowtail best,' said Phil. 'And look, look – there it is, on that leafy branch! Isn't it beautiful!'

'Well, I like the blue morpho,' said Maddie. 'Isn't it the brightest, loveliest blue?'

We had to circle the whole enclosure until we suddenly spotted one, sucking at an orange slice.

'Hey, he likes orange juice and so do I!' cried Maddie.

It took me ages to pick a favourite. I liked them *all*. Well, I liked the brightly coloured ones better than the browny ones, but I didn't like to say so out loud in case I hurt their feelings. I was a bit irritated with Phil and Maddie – I might have chosen either the emerald swallowtail or the blue morpho as *my* favourite. But then I saw a picture of a small butterfly called a 'postman'.

I thought it was a very funny name for a butterfly. I knew exactly how Mick on my table at school would draw it.

Perhaps the postman butterfly had that name because most of its wings were bright pillar-box red, but they had very smart black edges, with two bright white spots on either side.

'I think the postman butterfly is my favourite. Quick, let's find him!' I said.

We circled the enclosure, looking carefully on every branch, every bush, every fruit stand. We saw lots and lots of butterflies, but there weren't many red-and-black ones.

'There's your postman, Tina!' said Grandad, pointing up high.

We peered upwards but I shook my head.

'It's not a postman, Grandad. It's too big. I know it's red and black, but look – it hasn't got any white spots.'

'Perhaps it's been using face cream,' said Gran. 'I'm sure it *is* your Mr Postman, Tina.'

I think she was getting a bit bored of butterflies.

'It's *not.*' I consulted the picture chart again. 'It's this one, look – "big billy". It's red and black, but hasn't got any spots. It's definitely big billy.'

'Can't he count as your favourite?' asked Gran.

'Well, I like him, but I think I like the postman better,' I said.

Gran sighed. We went around the enclosure one more time. We saw swallowtails and morphos aplenty, and a host of other different kinds, but we couldn't spot a single postman.

'I don't think there can be any postmen at all today, pet,' said Grandad.

'They're all out on their rounds,' said Gran. 'Come on – who wants an ice cream?'

'Me!' said Phil.

'Me!' said Maddie.

'Me – but can we look for a postman butterfly first?' I asked.

'We've looked and looked and looked,' said Phil.

'We've looked until our eyes are falling out,' said Maddie.

'Couldn't we have just *one* more look?' I begged.

So we walked all round the enclosure one more time. We looked up. We looked down. We looked through. We looked over. We looked everywhere.

We still didn't see a postman.

'Come on, we're really going to have to go now, Tina.' Gran took my hand and pulled me towards the exit. I looked up just as we were going through the dangling plastic strips – and there, just above me, perching on the EXIT sign, was a little bright red butterfly with black wingtips and two big white spots on either side.

'Oh! Oh, how wonderful! Look, look, look! It's my postman!' I cried.

It flew down towards me and circled my head once, as if it was saying hello. Then it flew off, and soon I couldn't see it any more.

I was so excited I felt my face going bright red, just like the postman. I was so hot I wouldn't put my jacket on even when we were outside in the cold. Gran got cross with me and Grandad tried to chase after me, but they couldn't catch me for ages. I spread my arms like wings and pretended I was flying, just like the postman.

When I went to sleep that night I dreamed that the butterflies were in our bedroom – emerald swallowtails, blue morphos, and *hundreds* of postman butterflies.

Chapter Eight

When I woke up, the butterflies were all gone. I remembered that Baby was gone too and I was very, very sad. My hand felt so empty now. I clutched my teddy but he didn't really help. I didn't want to feel his soft fur. I wanted my hard little Baby – her round head, her smooth arms, the swell of her tummy, the little indentations of her toes.

I wanted her sooooooo much that I started crying. Not loud crying so that Mum could hear and come running. Just quiet, miserable, head-in-my-pillow crying.

Phil heard. Maddie heard. They got into my bed, though it was a bit of a squeeze for the three of us. We were like a triplet sandwich. I was the jam.

I felt a bit better squashed up with my sisters, but I couldn't stop crying for a long time. And then, when I did, I still felt dreadfully snuffly and my head hurt.

I didn't feel any better at breakfast time. I didn't want to eat my fruit or yoghurt. I didn't want to eat my toast. I only sipped my juice.

'Oh dear, oh dear, what's the matter with you, Teeny Weeny?' asked Mum. 'You look a bit pale and red-eyed.' She felt my forehead. 'You're quite hot too. I hope you're not going down with anything. Maybe you'd better have a pyjama day today.'

When any of us have a cold or get sick, we stay in our pyjamas and Mum brings us our meals on a tray, and we do colouring or read in bed. I've had heaps more pyjama days than Phil and Maddie.

They don't like pyjama days. Maddie gets especially fidgety. I quite *like* pyjama days.

So I got to stay in bed all Sunday. It wasn't lonely one bit.

Phil and Maddie and I played with our Monster High dolls and our Barbies. We pretended that they went to different schools and were deadly rivals, and they ended up having a big fight.

Mum said they were getting a bit boisterous and I needed some peace and quiet. So Phil and Maddie went off to play by themselves while Mum read to me – three whole chapters.

Then she had to go and see to the Sunday dinner, so Dad came and played cards with me.

I had my Sunday dinner on a tray – Mum gave me a teeny portion but I could only eat one potato. And two beans. And three spoonfuls of ice cream.

Then I had a nap. I woke up feeling worse: my nose was really stuffed up now, and my throat hurt and I felt hot and shivery at the same time.

'Oh dear, oh dear,' said Mum. 'I'd better take your temperature.'

In the afternoon I got a bit moany and groany.

I had more ice cream for tea. I didn't want anything else.

Later I put on my dressing gown to go down and watch a DVD. I was allowed to choose my favourite, *Frozen*. I sat on Dad's lap. It was fine for a bit, but then I got all droopy.

'We'd better pop you back to bed,' said Mum.

'Never mind, sweetheart. I'm sure you'll be as right as rain in the morning,' said Dad.

'I'm not so sure,' said Mum. 'I think she got thoroughly chilled yesterday. It was a bit irresponsible of your parents trailing them all round the zoo on such a cold day.'

'For heaven's sake, it's not like it's the middle of winter!'

'There was a very cold wind – and you know how quick Tina is to catch cold,' said Mum. 'Look at her! I don't think she'd better go to school tomorrow.'

Oh! That cheered me up a bit, though I was careful to carry on looking mournful.

'I think I've caught a cold too,' said Maddie quickly. 'A-tishoo, a-tishoo – see!'

'And me. I'm sure my nose feels stuffed up,' said Phil. 'Perhaps we'd better all stay off school tomorrow.'

'Now look what you've started!' said Dad. 'You little monkeys! You're all going to school tomorrow even if you sneeze your heads off.'

Phil and Maddie were as right as rain in the morning, much to their annoyance. But I still wasn't very well. I couldn't breathe properly and I hurt all over. Mum bundled me up in two sweaters and two pairs of tights and my big winter coat and took me to the doctor's.

I like Dr Jessop. We're old friends.

'Mmm, that chest sounds a bit crackly,' she said. 'I think we'd better give you some medicine, Tina.'

'And do I have to go to school?' I asked in a tiny, poorly voice.

'I think you'd better have a day or two in bed,' said Dr Jessop.

So Mum and I went home, and I put on soft clean pyjamas while Mum put crisp clean sheets on my bed, and then I curled up in my nice clean nest and tried to go back to sleep.

It felt very strange to be in the bedroom all by myself, without the sounds of Phil's heavy breathing and Maddie tossing and turning. It was too quiet. I could just about hear Mum phoning her work to say she couldn't come in today and then opening and closing cupboards in the kitchen, but up here in my bedroom everything was still and silent.

I peeped out of my sheets. The three dolls on

the windowsill were all looking at me. Rosebud was glaring, holding her rose as if she hated it. She was missing Baby too.

I felt so bad I started crying, and then it went on and on until my soft clean pyjamas and my crisp clean sheets were all hot and tangled and horrible.

'Oh, darling,' said Mum, coming into the bedroom. 'You poor little pet! Why didn't you call me? Where does it hurt, baby?'

When she said 'baby', I started wailing even harder.

'I think we'd better call Dr Jessop again!' said Mum.

'I'm not crying . . . because I'm feeling rubbish . . . though I *am* feeling rubbish . . . I'm crying because . . . because I've been . . . very, very naughty!' I said in little sobby jerks.

'Oh dear! What have you done?' Mum still had her arms round me and she was holding me tight.

'I . . . I took Baby to school!' I wailed.

'Well, that *was* very naughty,' said Mum, but she wiped my eyes tenderly with a tissue, and helped me blow my nose. 'I did tell you not to take Baby to school. But never mind. No harm done.'

'Yes there is! Lots and lots of harm,' I wept. 'Selma got her and threw her down the toilet!'

'Oh my goodness! What a horrible girl. How dare she! She did it *deliberately*?'

'Yes she did.'

'Well, when I go and collect Phil and Maddie from school I'll have a fierce word with Selma and her mother!' said Mum indignantly.

'Oh, Mum, I don't think that's a good idea. Selma and her mum might be very fierce back!' I couldn't help imagining this encounter.

This haunted me for the rest of the day . . . though Mum was being very kind, even though I'd been so naughty.

She gave me tomato soup for lunch. She didn't mind when I left most of it. She still let me have ice cream for pudding.

Then she read to me again, and then I cuddled down to sleep and she stroked my forehead and sang to me as if I were still a little baby.

I went to sleep properly, and didn't even wake up when Mrs Richards from next door came to watch me while Mum went to collect my sisters from school.

But I couldn't help waking up when Maddie burst into the bedroom, Phil following closely behind.

'Hey, Tina, you'll never guess what!' said Maddie.

'Ssh, Maddie, I expect Tina's got a headache,' said Phil. 'But just wait till you hear, Tina!'

I was still sleepy and I *did* have a headache, but I needed to sit up straight away and find out what had happened.

'Is Mum OK?' I asked, wondering if Selma or Selma's mum really had flattened her.

'Yes – she's downstairs making Mrs Richards a cup of tea. And some smoothies for us, I hope, because I'm starving,' said Maddie. 'But listen, Tina. When Mum came to meet us, she went over to Selma's mum and started a row with her!'

'She didn't *start* a row – she was ever so polite at first, but in a sort of icy way,' said Phil. 'You know: *Excuse me, Mrs Johnson, I believe your little girl Selma took a small china doll belonging to my daughter Tina and flushed it down the lavatory last Friday.*'

'And Selma's mum said, *You what?* So Mum said it all over again. And Selma goes, *I never.* But she looked all worried and guilty, so you could tell she was fibbing. So you'll never ever guess what Selma's mum did!' said Maddie.

'She didn't thump Mum, did she?' I asked anxiously.

'No, silly! She thumped Selma,' said Phil.

'*Thumped* her?'

'Yes, hit her hard about her head – *whack, whack, whack!*' said Maddie.

This was so extraordinary that I forgot all about feeling ill and sat bolt upright in bed.

'But you can't hit children! Especially not your own little girl!'

'I know. It's not allowed. But she did it,' said Phil.

'She did it lots,' said Maddie. 'And Selma cried.'

'She cried, and we saw, and I think that made her cry more,' said Phil.

'Well, it was her fault,' said Maddie. 'She shouldn't have flushed Baby away. That was really mean.'

'But not really mean enough to make your own mum smack you about the head,' said Phil.

'I'm ever so glad our mum doesn't smack us,' I said.

I couldn't quite imagine it. Mum could get cross – very cross – but she'd never once smacked us, not even a little tap.

Dad could get cross too, but he'd never smacked us either.

Gran sometimes *said* she'd give us a smacked bottom when we were being very naughty, but she'd never actually done it.

Grandad never said it. He never got cross. Gran said he let us get away with blue murder.

When Mum brought up our smoothies on a tray, I said, 'Mum, did Selma *really* get smacked?'

'Yes, she did. And it was horrible. I wished I'd never said anything. I tried to stop Selma's mum but she wouldn't listen. She kept calling Selma horrible names too. Poor little Selma.'

It was weird to hear Selma called *poor* and *little*. Just for a minute it made me think of her differently.

'She's not *poor*, Mum,' said Phil.

'She's not *little* either – she's the tallest girl in the class,' Maddie pointed out.

'I dare say, but I still feel sorry for her, with a mum like that,' said Mum.

'She's still the meanest girl ever,' said Phil.

'Especially to Tina,' added Maddie.

'I know, and that's horrible,' said Mum, 'but I think she's mean because her mum is mean to her. Perhaps . . . perhaps if you three girls tried to be extra nice to Selma, then she'd start being nice back . . .'

'Maybe,' said Phil, very doubtfully.

'Or maybe not!' said Maddie. 'Excuse me saying so, Mum, but that's a totally daft idea. You don't know what Selma can be like.'

'Well, let's forget all about Selma now. Drink up your smoothies and then I think you'd better leave Tina in peace,' said Mum.

'No, she wants us with her, don't you, Tina?' said Phil.

'It must have been weird for her without us all day long,' said Maddie.

'Don't worry, Mum, we'll be very quiet,' said Phil.

'Like little mice,' said Maddie.

So Mum left us alone together. It was very cosy. They took turns reading to me in very soft, gentle voices.

Then Phil acted out *Goldilocks and the Three Bears* with Rosa and our teddies.

Maddie scooped Cheesepuff out of his cage so that he could come and say hello to me.

We're not really allowed to take the hamsters out of their cage – once they all darted away when we were stroking them and we had to play Hunt the Hamster all over the house.

Mum would have been *very* cross if she'd seen Cheesepuff cuddled up in bed with me. But she didn't come back and Cheesepuff didn't try to run away, so no one got into trouble. It felt so lovely holding warm, furry Cheesepuff that I thought I might be getting better.

Dad came home from work with a big bunch of grapes. 'These are for the invalid,' he said.

That was me. But of course I shared them with Phil and Maddie.

I didn't want much supper after that. I didn't even fancy ice cream. I felt a bit sick. And then I *was* sick.

'Oh dear, oh dear,' said Mum.

She settled me down to sleep early, with a bowl beside my bed just in case. I went to sleep for a bit, but then I woke up and was sick again. And again.

Then Dad had to sleep in my bed while I was tucked up in the big bed with Mum. This is usually a big treat, but it didn't make me feel any better.

I couldn't go to school in the morning. I wasn't just a bit poorly. I was really ill.

Chapter Nine

It was just a cold at first, but then it went to my chest. When I saw Dr Jessop again, she murmured to Mum that I had a really nasty flu virus and she was worried I might be developing a touch of pneumonia. That's the most interesting word. I've spelled it right, honestly. I asked Mum. *I* thought you'd spell it *newmoanier*.

It certainly made me feel full of new moans. My chest hurt and my head hurt, and my arms and legs hurt. In fact *all* of me hurt.

I had to stay in bed all the time and take some big pills that nearly got stuck in my throat.

Mum stayed at home with me the first week. She read to me.

But then she'd used up all her leave and had to go back to work.

Dad stayed at home with me for a few days. He read to me too. He didn't always read out of a book.

Gran came too. But she insisted that Dad move Nibbles and Speedy and Cheesepuff out of the room. They squeaked indignantly. Then Gran squeaked, because she was rearranging Rosa and Primrose and Rosebud on the windowsill and saw that Rosebud was holding one flower instead of her little china baby.

Gran didn't get cross with me. She got cross with Mum later, when she came back from collecting Phil and Maddie.

'You should never have let Tina take that little dolly to school! You might have known she'd lose it,' said Gran, going *tut-tut-tut* with her teeth.

Gran and Mum looked like they were going to get into a real argument.

Phil nudged me. 'Groan, Tina,' she hissed.

So I groaned a lot, and Mum and Gran came running to my bed, all concerned, and by the time they'd fetched me a cold flannel for my hot head and an extra quilt for my shivery body they'd forgotten all about Baby and their argument.

Gran came back the next day with her beauty case. She works part time as a manicurist. She did her own nails, and then, when they were dry, she did mine! I didn't have to sit up in bed. I just had to poke my hands out on top of the duvet. Gran gave me the most amazing nails, with sparkly bits and little smiles. I couldn't help smiling too, even though I was so poorly.

Phil and Maddie were sooooo envious when they came home from school.

But most of the time Grandad looked after me. He only had a little job nowadays, delivering newspapers early in the morning.

'Funny, that,' he said. 'My very first job was delivering newspapers too.'

When Grandad got back from his newspaper round he'd have a little flop on Phil or Maddie's bed. He said he was just resting his eyes, but he sometimes snored. I rested my eyes too. I don't think *I* snored.

We both woke up in the middle of the morning.

'Time for elevenses,' said Grandad.

Sometimes it wasn't exactly eleven o'clock, so he'd say, 'Time for twenty-five-past-tensies,' or, 'Time for ten-to-elevensies.'

He'd go down to the kitchen and make us both a mug of hot chocolate with whipped cream and a marshmallow on top.

'It's naughty but it's nice,' he said.

He always drank his all up. Mostly I just had a couple of sips of mine, but I managed to eat the marshmallow.

Then Grandad would make me up my very

own story. Not a Phil-and-Maddie-and-me story. This was a story about Tina the Butterfly Princess. She didn't look a bit like all the other princes and princesses. She was a teeny weeny girl who slept in a walnut shell when she was a baby. She was bright green all over, which attracted a lot of rude comments. The King and Queen were very worried, but the nurse simply wrapped the strange green baby up in a big cocoon in the royal nursery. Tina slept and slept – until one day she burst out of the cocoon and spread out beautiful wings. She wasn't a little girl princess any more. She was a butterfly princess. She flew all over the royal gardens, daintily landing on flower after flower, while everyone marvelled. I loved loved loved my Butterfly Princess story.

After that I'd have another nap while Grandad read his newspaper.

Then Grandad would fix lunch. He got worried when

I didn't feel like eating anything. 'Perhaps we'd better try you on nectar. Isn't that what butterflies eat?' he said.

He made me teeny-tiny bite-sized sandwiches of bread and butter and honey. 'Honey's a bit like nectar,' he said.

He served them on my doll's tea-set china. They looked so pretty I had to eat one. And two more. Grandad was very pleased with me. In the afternoon I had another sleep. I seemed to be doing nothing *but* sleep.

'That's right, you're our little Sleeping Beauty,' said Grandad. 'Sleep's good for you, pet.'

I certainly knew that Grandad was good for me.

Dr Jessop's pills worked and the pneumonia went away, but I was still very weak and droopy.

'You need bed rest, Tina. You can't go back to school yet – not for another week at least,' said Dr Jessop.

'You lucky, lucky thing, Tina!' said Phil and Maddie.

Then someone very surprising came to visit.

I heard the knock on the front door. I heard

Mum and Phil and Maddie. I knew by the sound of their voices that they were very surprised.

There was a lot of talk downstairs, and then I heard Mum say, 'I'll take you up to see Tina.'

I wondered who it could be. I was sure it wasn't Gran or Grandad. Maybe it was Mrs Richards?

I practically fell out of bed when Mum brought *Miss Lovejoy* into my bedroom! Was she going to tell me off for staying away from school for so long?

'Don't look so worried, Tina, I'm only here on a fleeting visit,' said Miss Lovejoy. 'I just came to see how you are. Philippa and Madeleine have been keeping me up to date with the news. I gather you're on the mend now.'

I nodded.

'You still don't look very well, dear.'

Dear!!!

'I'm glad you're being looked after so well. I know you won't be back to school for a little while, so I've brought you a few books and your exercise books – you can do a bit of catching up when you feel like it.' Miss Lovejoy put a very big heavy carrier bag on the end of my bed.

When I felt like it??? I didn't *ever* feel like doing multiplication or learning spellings, even when I was well. And that carrier bag looked chock-a-block with homework.

'What do you say, Tina?' said Mum. 'It's very kind of Miss Lovejoy to come here, isn't it?'

I gave a little nod again. 'Thank you, Miss Lovejoy,' I mumbled.

Miss Lovejoy sat down beside me on the bed.

It felt weird having her so close.

'We're all missing you, you know,' she said. She paused. 'Even Selma seems a bit woebegone.'

I was astonished.

'Perhaps she just misses having someone to tease,' said Miss Lovejoy. 'Anyway, the class have all written you Get Well Soon letters. They're in the carrier too.'

'*Selma's* written me a Get Well letter?' I asked.

'Yes – every single member of the class.'

'Even Phil and Maddie?'

'Yes. I told them not to tell you. I wanted it to be a lovely surprise,' said Miss Lovejoy. 'Well, you rest as much as you can and get completely better.'

She gave my hand a little pat, just like a fond auntie, and then she let Mum see her out of the house.

Phil and Maddie came charging into the room.

'Wow! Fancy Miss Lovejoy coming to visit you. She never said she was going to,' said Phil.

'Did she give you the letters? We all had to do one. It was weird writing a letter to you, Tina,' said Maddie.

'Did she tell you off at all?' asked Phil.

'No. No, she was actually quite nice. She called me "dear" and patted my hand,' I said, still stunned.

'She never!' said Maddie. 'It can't have been *our* Miss Lovejoy. It must have been her much nicer twin sister.'

'She did bring me heaps of school stuff though,' I said, sighing.

I wriggled along to the end of the bed and started delving in the carrier bag. There were school books and my project books and exercise books. I sighed.

Then I found a big folder of letters. Twenty-seven letters – one from everyone in the class. They'd all drawn a picture too. Some of them were of me in bed, looking poorly. Mick had given me hideous spots and a speech bubble saying, 'Phew! Moania.' Peter drew me so small that I looked like a little insect in weeny pyjamas. Alistair had drawn me like a medical illustration with arrows. One pointed to my forehead and said *High temperature*; another pointed to my arms and legs and said *Aches and pains*; one pointed to my tummy and said *Feeling sick*. He was the only one in the whole class who spelled *pneumonia* correctly.

Harry drew me completely well, and scoring a goal in a football match. I liked Harry's letter. I liked Neera's too. She drew all her brothers and sisters and her mum and dad, and even her granny and auntie, all saying *Get well soon, Tina!* I liked Phil's letter. She drew Nibbles and Speedy and Cheesepuff in little hamster beds, blowing their noses with tiny hankies, pretending they'd got hamster pneumonia. I liked Maddie's letter too. She drew the three of us together holding hands, but she drew me absolutely huge, my head almost off the page. She wrote: *You're going to get completely better, and so big and strong that you'll be the tallest of all three of us.*

There were only two letters I didn't like.

Kayleigh drew a very ugly pin-girl who didn't look anything like me and wrote one sentence: *Dear Tina, Get better, from Kayleigh.*

Selma did a rubbish picture too. She gave me cross-eyes and a crooked mouth, and made my arms and legs look like matchsticks. She wrote: *Dear Tina, I hope you get better soon. I can't wait till you can come back to school. From Selma.*

I can't wait till you can come back to school . . .

I knew what that meant all right. *I can't wait to GET you!*

I scrumpled Selma's letter up and stuffed it back in the carrier bag. There was still something else down at the bottom. It was a bulky parcel wrapped up in pretty paper and tied with a blue ribbon. There was a small card attached to it, which said: *A little present from Miss Lovejoy.*

'Miss Lovejoy's given you a *present?*' said Phil.

'Open it, quick!' said Maddie. 'I bet it's a spelling book or maths tables – something ultra-boring like that.'

It wasn't at all boring. It was a wonderful present. It was a little book all about butterflies, a proper grown-up sketchpad, and a tin of colouring pencils.

Chapter Ten

I opened up my new drawing book straight after breakfast the next day. I knew exactly what I was going to draw: I was going to do a whole book of butterflies.

I looked in the butterfly book Miss Lovejoy had given me. I wanted to copy each butterfly carefully and get its markings exactly right. I looked for a postman first. I couldn't find one. Then I looked for an emerald swallowtail. No luck either. I tried searching for a blue morpho, but there wasn't one.

I couldn't help thinking that Miss Lovejoy's book wasn't much good. I closed it with a snap.

'Have you got fed up already?' asked Grandad.

'Yes! I can't find any of the really good butterflies. There's no postman!' I said crossly. 'No emerald swallowtail, no blue morpho. This is a rubbish book.'

'Hey, hey, calm down, madam. I can tell you're getting better – you're in a right stroppy mood,' said Grandad, chuckling.

He picked up my book and flicked through it. 'Here, isn't this a blue whatsit?' he said.

I peered. 'Oh. It *is* a pretty blue, but it isn't a blue morpho – it says it's an Adonis blue. I do like it though. I'll draw that one first.'

'You know what?' said Grandad. 'We're both a bit thick, Tina. This is a book about *British* butterflies. Your Mr Postman and the other two came from Africa. You can only see those butterflies in special enclosures. But maybe you'll get to see *these* butterflies flying about the garden.'

'Oh, I do hope so!' I said.

I settled to drawing my Adonis blue butterfly, and then I selected the bright blue pencil from my tin. I coloured it in ever so carefully, making the blue darker near the wing tips, and leaving a white fringe all round the edges of the wings. Even the Adonis blue's body was blue and very furry. It was just like Gran's blue fun fur jacket.

I read all about Adonis blue butterflies, pointing along with my finger because the print was quite small. Then I carefully printed the following underneath my Adonis blue:

I feel sorry for the females because they are chocolate brown and nowhere near as pretty. They live in chalk grasslands. They like to eat marjoram and ragwort.

I was very careful to copy the spellings properly because I wanted my butterfly book to be perfect.

'Where are there chalk grasslands, Grandad?' I asked.

'Mm, let's think ... *I* know. Your gran and I used to climb up Box Hill when we were courting. We went up a little chalky path – it was ever so slippy! And there was certainly grass everywhere. Perhaps that's your chalk grasslands.'

'Will you take me when I'm better?'

'I think that path might be too much of a struggle for you, pet. And I'm pretty sure I'd never manage it nowadays.'

'We could try,' I said determinedly. 'What's marge-or-am, Grandad?'

'Not sure, pet. I think it's some kind of herb. You use it for flavouring in cooking, if you're into fancy food.'

'What's ragwort?'

'Maybe that's a herb too. Or a weed? *Little Weed!*' Grandad said 'Little Weed' in a funny voice. Little Weed was in a television programme he used to watch when he was little. There were

Flower Pot Men in that programme too. They spoke in even funnier voices. Grandad likes to pretend to be them as well.

We watched some of the CBeebies programmes I used to like when *I* was little. There was a new one I'd never seen before called *Ruby Red*. This funny lady, Ruby, dressed up  as lots of different people. She even dressed up as a cat and licked milk out of a bowl, and then she was a donkey with big ears going 'Hee-haw, hee-haw.' She didn't have proper costumes, but she was so good at acting you really believed she had turned into all these people and animals.

I'd have loved Ruby Red when I was little. I liked her a lot now.

After lunch (bite-sized pieces of cheese on toast and weeny carrot sticks served on my doll's tea set) I had a nap, and then Grandad said he had a big surprise. He had to go downstairs to fetch it, then staggered back into the bedroom with an enormous box of Lego.

'It's a treat for all you girls, but I thought you and I could make a start on it this afternoon, eh, Tina?' he said.

We had a lovely afternoon starting to build Tower Bridge.

I got tired after a bit, but Grandad didn't.

We all did a bit of building when Mum and Dad and Phil and Maddie came home.

So this was my new life, day after day. I had stories and treat meals and cuddles and television, and we did *lots* of Lego-building.

I nearly forgot about school. Once or twice I looked at the school books Miss Lovejoy had brought me, but then I popped them back in their bag. I didn't feel like writing about the Ancient Egyptians, however you spelled them, and I certainly didn't want to do any spelling or sums.

But I *did* draw lots of butterflies.

I drew a brimstone – a male one so I could colour it in bright yellow, with an orange spot on each wing.

This is a male brimstone. The females are much paler, poor things. They live in woodland glades and hedgerows. They live on nectar from buddleia.

I drew a large white and a small white butterfly.

This is a large white and a small white butterfly. They like to live in gardens with cabbages! When they are caterpillars they LOVE eating cabbage (I hate it).

I drew a small tortoiseshell butterfly.

This is a small tortoise-shell. They like to live in flowery gardens. I wish we had one! They like to sip the juice from apples and pears.

I drew a meadow brown butterfly.

This is a meadow brown butterfly. They live all over the place, in grass and gardens. They eat nectar from all different flowers. I like their eye spots.

I drew a large skipper butterfly.

This is a large skipper. It isn't VERY large. It lives in parks and hedges. The male large skippers like to chase away other males. I know lots of boys like that.

I drew a red admiral.

This is a red admiral. They live in gardens and meadows. They feed off flowers and fruit juice. They are very speedy.

I drew a green hairstreak.

This is a green hairstreak. They live all over the place in hedges, moors, hills, heaths and wasteland. They like all kinds of flowers. They rest with their wings closed. This is sensible because they can't be easily spotted.

I drew a peacock all over again, but this time it was even better than the one I did for Miss Lovejoy. I drew its antennae properly. These are the sticking-out bits on its head so it can smell and touch. I divided its body carefully, making the top thorax hairy and the abdomen stripy. I wished *I* had a hairy chest and a stripy tummy.

This is a peacock butterfly. They like flowery gardens and meadows. They eat nectar from flowers and juice from fruit. My teacher has my drawing of another peacock butterfly up on her wall!

'My word, you've been a busy bee,' said Grandad, flipping through my drawing book. 'Or should I say busy *butterfly*?'

Grandad had been busy too. He had built an enormous Tower Bridge in our bedroom. He did nearly all of it himself, though he let me put in the last few bricks. There was hardly room to move in our bedroom now.

'We'll keep it until Monday, when Tina goes back to school,' Mum said when she saw it. 'Then we'll have to break it up and put all the bricks back in the box.'

'That's a shame,' said Grandad. 'Oh well. Maybe I'll take Tower Bridge home with me and build it all over again.'

'No you won't!' said Gran, who'd popped over after work to see how I was.

I wondered how I was. I didn't feel sick or headachey any more. My chest didn't hurt and I hardly ever coughed. I didn't feel wobbly when I stood up. I was eating almost normally. In fact, I could manage a *big* bowl of ice cream now. So was I really better? Well enough to go back to school on Monday like Mum said?

I thought about school. I thought about Selma.

'I don't feel very well,' I said in a tiny voice. I hung my head and went all floppy. 'I don't think I'm ready to go back to school yet.'

Mum looked at me carefully. She felt my forehead. 'I think you're right as rain, young lady. School on Monday!'

On Sunday night I dreamed I was back at school and Selma had grown much, much bigger – ten times bigger than me. She picked me up and Phil and Maddie couldn't stop her. Even Miss Lovejoy couldn't stop her. Selma just pushed them out of her way with one massive hand, keeping tight hold of me with the other. She marched me out of the classroom, down the corridor and into the toilets.

Then she opened a cubicle door and threw me into the lavatory and *pulled the chain*.

I truly didn't feel very well on Monday morning. I wouldn't get up when Mum called. I didn't eat any breakfast. I cried when Mum told me off.

'Now, lovey, this simply won't do,' she said, pulling me close and giving me a hug. 'You really are better now. You have to go to school today. You can't stay home for ever.'

'Why can't I?' I wept.

'You know why, silly. It's the law that all little girls have to go to school.'

'I'll break the law. I'll go to prison. I'd *sooner* go to prison than to school,' I declared.

'It would be *me* going to prison, silly, for not sending you,' said Mum.

'You can't put our own mother in prison, Tina!' Phil put her arm round me. 'Don't worry about Selma.'

'Phil and I told her that you were very, very ill and it was all because she pushed you and upset you,' said Maddie. 'That shut her up a bit!'

'Yes, she's been much quieter ever since.

She hasn't done anything horrid to us at all,' said Phil.

'I think she'll still do horrid things to me,' I said.

'Well, I won't let her. And Harry won't either,' said Maddie. 'I told him what Selma did to Baby, and he said that if she ever tries any tricks like that again he'll gang up on her with all the boys. That's half the class! She'll be powerless then.'

'I think Selma could beat half the class, easy-peasy,' I said.

'And I told Neera, and I know she'll look after you too, *and* all the girls on my table,' said Maddie.

'And *I'm* going to look after you because I'm your mum and I love you very much,' said Mum. 'So much that I'm prepared to do battle with Miss Lovejoy all over again and have you put on another table altogether if it kills me!'

I felt a little bit cheered up with all this support. I got ready for school and put all the books and pads Miss Lovejoy had brought me in my satchel. I felt worried all over again. I hadn't got round to doing *any* work. I hung my head. 'Miss Lovejoy's going to be cross with me!' I said.

'No she won't. I'm sure she'll understand that you just didn't feel well enough,' said Mum. 'Tell you what – take your drawing book to school too. Show her all those lovely butterflies you drew.'

So I put my butterfly drawing book in my satchel too. But I still felt very, very scared as we walked to school. I felt as if all my butterflies were in my tummy, fluttering around.

Chapter Eleven

I spotted Selma the moment I got into the playground. She spotted me too. She was glaring. I clutched at Mum. I wanted her to pick me up even though I knew I was being a baby.

Then Neera came running over. 'Hi, Phil,' she said, and they did a funny hello thing with their hands – a bit like a high five but more elaborate.

'What are they doing?' I asked Maddie.

'Oh, they're in this funny

club thing,' she told me. 'They have secret codes and passwords and they make badges.'

'Aren't you in their club too?' said Mum.

'It's really just for people on their table. I don't mind,' Maddie said cheerfully. 'I'd sooner go and play footie with Harry and the boys.'

'Well, I really want both of you to look after Tina today,' said Mum.

'She can play with us,' said Maddie.

'You know she's not allowed to play football.'

'She can be the ref. I'll get Harry to lend her his whistle.'

'Or she can be in our club. We'll let her join because she's my sister and she's been poorly,' said Phil. 'It's breaking the rules, but it doesn't matter, because Neera and I are the ones who made them all up.'

'Well, which would you prefer, Tina?' said Mum.

I didn't prefer *either* option. I liked football, but I didn't know the rules and couldn't be bothered to learn them. I didn't see how I could be a ref (though I rather liked the idea of blowing the whistle).

I liked clubs but I knew I'd forget all these codes and passwords (though I wouldn't have minded a badge).

I didn't say anything. I just bent my head.

'I think just until Tina finds her feet again at school it would be better if you played together nicely, the three of you,' said Mum. 'Now, let's go in and see Miss Lovejoy.'

We had to go past Selma. I hung onto Mum's hand tightly. Phil went first. She ignored Selma altogether. Then Maddie went by. She gave Selma a fierce look.

'Hello, Selma,' said Mum.

Selma turned her back.

'Here's Tina, back at school again,' Mum went on.

Selma started to walk away.

'Selma? I'm talking to you!'

Selma stood still, hunched over.

'I do hope that you and Tina can learn to play nicely together,' said Mum.

Phil and Maddie and I looked at each other. Phil and Maddie rolled their eyes. As if Selma would ever play nicely with anyone!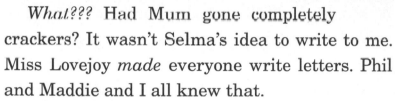

'Tina was very touched to get your letter, Selma,' said Mum.

What??? Had Mum gone completely crackers? It wasn't Selma's idea to write to me. Miss Lovejoy *made* everyone write letters. Phil and Maddie and I all knew that.

'Mum!' Phil hissed.

'Selma didn't *want* to write a letter,' said Maddie.

'But it was a lovely thing to do all the same,' said Mum. 'Well done, Selma!'

Then she hurried us into school.

'Why are you being all nicey-nice to *Selma*, Mum?' asked Phil.

'She's our deadly enemy!' said Maddie. 'She's the meanest girl in our class. In the whole school. In the whole city. In the whole country. In the whole universe!'

'But perhaps if everyone was a bit kinder to Selma, she might stop being so mean,' said Mum. 'I don't think she has a very happy time at home. Remember how her mum slapped her?'

'*I'd* slap Selma, given half a chance,' said Maddie.

I didn't say anything. I was too busy being worried. I hated the smell of school and the sound of school. I shut my eyes and wished wished wished that I was back home in bed drawing butterflies.

Miss Lovejoy was at her desk. She frowned when Mum opened the classroom door – but then she smiled a bit when she saw that it was us.

'Hello, Mrs Maynard. Hello, Philippa and Madeleine. And hello, Tina! Welcome back to school! I'm so pleased to see you.'

Mum gave me a little nudge. I didn't know what to do. I couldn't possibly say I was pleased to see Miss Lovejoy because it would have been a great big fib.

'Tina's feeling a little overwhelmed at the moment, Miss Lovejoy,' said Mum.

'Of course. That's entirely understandable. Don't worry, I'll keep my eye on her,' said Miss Lovejoy.

Oh dear. I didn't want Miss Lovejoy's beady eye on me, thank you!

'That's very kind of you.' Mum took a deep breath. 'I know you want to keep my girls separated in class, but I was wondering . . . Would it be possible for Tina to sit with one or other of her sisters for a few days, just until she gets used to school again?'

'Well,' said Miss Lovejoy, lacing her fingers and looking at Mum over her glasses, 'I've given it some thought, but I'm not sure it would be good for Tina in the long run. She has to learn to stand on her own two feet – even though they're a bit wobbly at the moment.'

'Could she at least change to a different table?' said Mum.

'I've considered that too. But if I let Tina sit on another table, then I'll have half the class wanting to swap places. However, I don't want you to think I'm too hard-hearted. I've rearranged

Tina's table. She's sitting between Michael and Alistair now, and they're both good-hearted boys. They'll be little gentlemen and look after her. Don't worry, Mrs Maynard. Tina will be fine.'

Mum still looked worried. So did Phil and Maddie. And I was very, very, very worried.

Chapter Twelve

So I sat at the same table, though *not* next to Selma.

She could still kick me under the table, but she had to slide right down in her seat to do it. Whenever Miss Lovejoy saw her slipping downwards, she said, 'Come along, Selma, sit up properly.'

She wasn't near enough to nudge or poke me and she couldn't reach to scribble all over my drawings. It was sooooo much better. And it was actually quite good to sit between Mick and Alistair.

Mick was my second favourite boy in the class after Harry. He could be very funny. I loved watching him in dance and drama. He made us all roar with laughter when we were pretending to be dogs.

Alistair was never funny. He was the most serious person I'd ever met. But it was very useful sitting next to him because he knew all the answers and didn't mind if you copied a bit.

He helped me catch up on all the work I'd missed. Miss Lovejoy nearly got cross when she saw I hadn't done any homework at all.

'There now! And I made all that effort to come over to your house to give you work so you wouldn't fall behind,' she said, shaking her head at me. 'You're a naughty, lazy girl, Tina Maynard.'

'I'm naughty but I'm not lazy, Miss Lovejoy,' I said. 'I did do lots of work in my butterfly book. Do you want to look at it?'

'Not just now. This is a maths lesson and you must practise your multiplication sums,' she said in a stern voice.

I hadn't got to grips with multiplication before I got ill. I couldn't work out how to do it at all.

I went up to Miss Lovejoy's desk and she showed me very simple multiplication sums. They were still too difficult for me and I didn't understand, but I didn't dare tell her in case she got even crosser.

I went back to my seat and looked at the three sums she'd set me, but I couldn't do them at all. I bent my head over my book, feeling sick. I gave little moans, and Phil and Maddie heard.

'Please, Miss Lovejoy, Tina doesn't look very well,' said Phil.

'She's gone all green. That means she's going to be sick,' said Maddie. 'Can we take her out to the toilets?'

Miss Lovejoy looked at me carefully. 'I don't think she's sick. I think she's simply sick of hard work,' she said. 'Have you finished those sums yet, Tina?'

'Not quite, Miss Lovejoy.' I started sniffling.

'Haven't you got a clean tissue?' said Alistair. 'Hang on, I've got a packet in my pocket. Have you still got pneumonia? I hope not!'

'I'm just crying a little bit,' I whispered. 'Don't tell or Selma will call me a baby.'

'Why are you crying?' he asked in his clear loud voice.

'Ssh! Because I can't do my sums.'

'But they're easy-peasy.'

'They are for *you*.'

'Look, shall I show you how to do them?' He leaned over and showed me. He did it again. And again. Then he rubbed out the answer and made *me* do it.

'That's right!'

'Miss Lovejoy, Alistair's doing all Tina's sums,' said Selma.

'Is that right, Alistair?' asked Miss Lovejoy.

'I'm *helping* her, but she's just done a sum all by herself, Miss Lovejoy,' said Alistair.

'Then that's good,' said Miss Lovejoy. 'I don't need a teacher's assistant in this class while I have you, Alistair.'

Phil and Maddie came and played with me at break time and lunch time. They were very kind and chose all my favourite games. We were princesses, and then we were witches, and then we were mermaids, and then we were knights fighting dragons.

The games weren't quite as good as usual though. Phil kept looking over at Neera and her friends, who were sitting in a circle writing in exercise books. Maddie kept staring at Harry and the other boys playing football.

I wondered about telling Phil that she could go and join Neera and the other members of her club. I wondered about telling Maddie that she could go and play football with Harry. But if I did that, who would I play with?

Everyone in our class seemed to be in little gangs and groups. Even Kayleigh had friends now because she was good at dancing.

There was only one girl in our class who didn't have anyone to play with.

And I *certainly* wasn't going to play with Selma.

I was still so scared of her

that I didn't want to go to the toilet just in case she came after me. I decided I simply wouldn't go.

'What's the matter, Tina?' said Phil.

'Nothing,' I said.

'Yes there is,' said Maddie. 'You keep fidgeting.'

'I'm fine,' I said, though I wasn't.

'You need to go to the loo!' said Phil.

'No I don't,' I lied.

'Go on, quick, before the bell goes,' said Maddie.

'I don't *need* to go,' I protested.

'Would you like us to come with you?' asked Phil.

'Yes!' I said.

So my sisters escorted me, one on either side, and waited outside the door while I went. I was only *just* in time. And while I was washing my hands Selma came in.

'Oh help,' I said.

'It's all right, we're here,' said Phil.

'What do *you* want?' Maddie asked Selma.

'What do you think?' she said. 'Is there some law says I can't use these toilets? Or do you stuck-up rubbish triplets actually *own* them? Are you about to start charging a penny a wee?'

'We'd charge *you* a whole pound!' said Phil.

'You owe us far more than a pound. You chucked my sister's valuable china doll down the loo. I bet it cost our gran heaps and heaps,' said Maddie.

'Baby!' I said, suddenly overcome with longing for her. I thought of her tumbling wretchedly through mile after mile of terrible stinking sewage, and burst out crying.

'There! Look! You've made my sister cry!' said Phil.

'She's just a spoiled little cry-baby,' said Selma. 'Boo-hoo, boo-hoo!'

'You shut up. Our sister's been ill. It's very serious when you get pneumonia,' said Maddie. 'She could have *died*. Don't you dare upset her now! You say another word and I'll punch you right in the face!'

'Maddie!' Phil squeaked. 'Don't! You mustn't fight!'

'Ooh, *mustn't be naughty and fight*!' said Selma in a silly voice. 'Or maybe you're just chicken.' She made *cluck-cluck-cluck* noises.

'I'm not chicken!' Maddie squared up to Selma, her fists clenched.

'Don't, Maddie!' Phil begged.

'Don't, don't, don't!' I cried.

Selma was much taller than Maddie. She was much stronger than Maddie. She was much fiercer than Maddie.

We all knew that Maddie couldn't possibly beat Selma in any kind of fight. But then, thank goodness, thank goodness, the bell rang, and one of the Year Six monitors came dashing in.

'Off to your classroom, you lot! Go on, don't stand there gawping. Didn't you hear the bell?'

'I need to use the toilet,' said Selma, and locked herself into a cubicle.

'We don't!' said Phil, and she hurried us away.

'I thought you said Selma was better?' I said, rubbing my eyes. 'She's *worse*!'

'I wish that bell hadn't gone,' said Maddie. 'I'd have punched her and punched her otherwise.'

Phil and I looked at each other. We didn't say anything.

Selma was five minutes late for afternoon lessons.

'Selma! What on earth have you been doing?' asked Miss Lovejoy.

'Nothing,' Selma mumbled. She was rubbing her eyes too. It almost looked as if *she'd* been crying, but of course that was impossible. Great big tough girls like Selma never cried.

It was art now, my favourite lesson. Miss Lovejoy showed us a picture of a big vase of yellow sunflowers, the colours so bright they made you blink.

'Now I want *you* to paint sunflowers, children,' she said.

I thought, *Goody-goody-goody*, but to my HUGE annoyance Miss Lovejoy said I had to copy some of the lessons I'd missed out of Alistair's exercise books.

'But I really, really, really want to paint some sunflowers!' I said.

'I know, and I'm sure you'd be very good at it, Tina. But you need to catch up on all those lessons you missed. You should have tried to do a little more work when you were at home,' said Miss Lovejoy.

'It's not fair,' I mumbled.

'Life isn't fair, Tina. Now settle down and stop moaning.'

So I had to sit there copying while everyone else splashed yellow paint about and created beautiful sunflowers.

'*Miss Lovejoy is mean mean mean mean mean,*' I muttered under my breath.

'Are you humming, Tina?' asked Miss Lovejoy. 'Be quiet now.'

I copied and copied and copied. I got sick of the sight of Alistair's squiggly writing. He used such long words too, just like a textbook. By the end of the afternoon it felt as if his loud pompous voice were spouting facts inside my head.

While everyone else was clearing up the paint things, Miss Lovejoy beckoned me over to her desk. She glanced at all my copying. 'Well done, Tina. You've worked very hard to catch up.'

'I'm not going to have to do copying every art lesson, am I, Miss Lovejoy?' I asked plaintively.

'No, of course not,' she said. 'Now, how about showing me the drawings you did at home?'

I went and fetched the sketchbook from my satchel. I felt suddenly shy and worried. I'd loved drawing and colouring all my butterflies. I didn't want Miss Lovejoy telling me I'd drawn a wing wrong or made a spelling mistake.

She turned page after page, not saying a word. I waited, fidgeting. Then she looked up and smiled at me. A really big smile. 'Oh, Tina!' she said.

'Isn't it good, Miss Lovejoy?' said Phil, coming to stand beside me.

'She did it all by herself, Miss Lovejoy,' said Maddie. 'She's ever so good at drawing, isn't she?'

'Yes, she is,' agreed Miss Lovejoy. 'And you've written some very interesting facts about butterflies too.'

'I *like* butterflies,' I said.

'In the spring you'll be able to look out for all these butterflies in your garden.'

'We haven't got a proper garden,' I said.

'We just have pebbly bits like a beach at the front,' said Phil.

'And a yard at the back with our trampoline and the barbecue stuff,' said Maddie.

'Well, perhaps your grandma and grandpa have a garden?' said Miss Lovejoy.

'No, they live in a flat,' Phil told her.

'Well, I'll have to put my thinking cap on,' she said.

I didn't quite understand. I thought Miss Lovejoy meant a real cap, like

or   or

I didn't realize she meant that she was going to think very hard about a butterfly garden.

Chapter Thirteen

When the bell rang for playtime the next day, Miss Lovejoy clapped her hands.

'Wait a minute, everyone. I need a couple of children to do some hard work for me this playtime. All right, who likes football?'

'Me!'

'Me!'

'Me!'

Lots of 'Me!'s. Nearly all the boys and half the girls said 'Me!' Maddie said 'Me!' the loudest, even louder than Harry.

'Well, you're getting good exercise already, so

out you go into the playground and start your football match.' Miss Lovejoy made shooing motions with her hands.

Maddie rushed to the door – and then hung back.

'Yes, Madeleine?' said Miss Lovejoy.

'I don't know what to do!' she said. 'I like football, but I like playing with Phil and Tina too.'

'I think they're going to be preoccupied with other things. Don't worry about Tina. She'll be busy doing work with me.'

'Oh!' Maddie looked at me, her head on one side, mouthing, *Is that all right?*

I didn't know whether to shake my head or nod. While I was making up my mind, she went out of the classroom.

'Now, I know some of you like dancing too,' said Miss Lovejoy. 'That's also very good exercise. So you go out into the playground and practise your dance steps.'

Kayleigh and five other girls went out – Sarah, Lucy, Princess, Danka and Nell. Selma stood up too, looking uncertain.

'Are you good at dancing, Selma?' asked Miss Lovejoy.

'No, she's rubbish at it,' Sarah whispered to the others, and they all giggled. It was true. We'd had a country dancing lesson that morning. We had to have partners. Phil and Maddie both ran over to me and said that we three would dance together, but Miss Lovejoy said we were being silly. We had to be in partners of two, one girl and one boy.

Phil danced with a boy on her table called Mark.

Maddie danced with Harry, lucky thing.

I ended up dancing with Alistair. I discovered that dancing was the only thing Alistair wasn't good at. He kept treading on my toes and starting with the left foot instead of the right. He went very red in the face.

'I hate this silly dancing,' he muttered.

Selma was even worse. She was dancing with Mick. He was all bouncy-bouncy to the music, but she was stiff and kept stepping the wrong way. She got angry and tried to make out it was all Mick's fault, but he just laughed at her.

Selma must have known she was bad at dancing, but she didn't like the others saying so. She glared and glared.

'I don't think you're especially fond of dancing, Selma,' said Miss Lovejoy, 'so you wait in the classroom, please. Now, I have a feeling that some of you are in special clubs – is that right?'

Phil and her friends giggled and nudged each other.

'I like it that you've had the initiative to start up a club. I'm sure you have special club business to attend to, so off you go,' said Miss Lovejoy.

Phil hung back. 'I think I'll stay with Tina,' she said.

'Oh, Phil, you're the one who makes up all the rules!' Neera told her. 'You have to come too.'

Phil peered at me. I mouthed *Stay!* at her, because there were only two other girls left in the classroom. One of them was me, and the other was Selma!

'Run along, Philippa,' said Miss Lovejoy. 'Don't look so worried. *I'll* be staying with Tina.'

She still looked very anxious.

'Off you go!'

Phil went. Selma and I were left together.

'Now then . . .' Miss Lovejoy went to her store cupboard.

Selma pulled a hideous face at me. 'Poor lickle-wickle cry-baby buggy-wuggy,' she muttered. 'You wait!'

I had to wait. I wasn't at all happy.

Miss Lovejoy emerged from the store cupboard with two painting overalls. 'Put these on, girls,' she said.

'Oh! Are we going to do painting?' I said, perking up a little. 'Can I do some sunflowers?'

'No, we're not doing painting, Tina. We're going to do a spot of manual labour and I don't want you to get your school clothes grubby.'

Manual labour? What did she mean?

She was delving around in a carrier bag now. She took out three things wrapped in newspaper: three *spades* – one big and two smaller ones.

'What are them spades for?' asked Selma.

'What are *those* spades for, *Miss Lovejoy*,' said Miss Lovejoy. 'What do you *think* spades are for, Selma? Digging!'

'Where are we going to dig, Miss Lovejoy?' I couldn't think of anywhere to dig at school. Unless . . . 'Are we going to dig in the sandpit?'

'I'm not playing with all them babies,' said Selma.

'*Those* babies, Selma. And rest assured, I don't want you to regress back to infancy,' said Miss Lovejoy. 'You're going to do some proper digging. Come with me, girls.'

She gave us each a spade and we followed along after her, down the corridor and out into the playground. We walked over the asphalt to the grassy patch at the end. It wasn't very grassy any more. There was lots of bare, greyish earth, a few weeds, and a lot of empty crisp packets and chocolate wrappers, even though it was strictly forbidden to chuck your litter away.

'Dear me!' exclaimed Miss Lovejoy. 'Here, Tina, you'd better be litter monitor. Gather every scrap and put it in the bag. Selma, you and I will make a start on the digging.'

'Why are we digging in this dirt?' asked Selma. 'Is it a punishment?'

'We're going to make a garden,' said Miss Lovejoy. 'A butterfly garden!'

'Oh!' I clapped my hands, dropping the chocolate wrappers I'd just picked up.

'I gather that's a clap of approval,' said Miss Lovejoy.

'Oh yes yes yes! Thank you so much, Miss Lovejoy! Oh, you're so kind! I'd love a butterfly garden more than anything!'

'I wouldn't!' said Selma. 'I don't even like stupid butterflies. Why should I get roped in? Let Tina do the digging if she wants a garden.'

'Very well,' said Miss Lovejoy.

We both stared at her.

'Leave the litter clearance for now. Get started on the digging, Tina.'

So I picked up my spade and started digging. Well, I tried. The spade wouldn't go into the ground properly. I tried again and again.

'Like this, Tina,' said Miss Lovejoy. She put her spade on the earth, and pressed down hard on the top of the blade with her stout shoe. 'You have to put a bit of effort in. Try to use your whole body strength.'

I tried – I really did. I put my foot on my spade

and shoved, then slipped sideways so that I fell over. It hurt a lot and normally I'd have cried, but this wasn't an option in front of Selma and Miss Lovejoy. I gritted my teeth and tried again, but I couldn't get the spade to go down far enough, no matter how I tried.

'She's useless,' Selma jeered.

'Yes, she is,' said Miss Lovejoy. 'But look how hard she's trying, Selma. She's gone bright red in the face. Have a little rest, Tina.'

I leaned against a tree thankfully.

'Why do you think Tina finds it so hard to dig, Selma?' asked Miss Lovejoy.

'Because she's useless,' said Selma.

'You've already said that. But *why* is she?'

'Because she's just a little squirt.'

'Yes, Tina's very little and very thin,' agreed Miss Lovejoy. 'And she's been very ill. She badly wants to make a butterfly garden but she needs some help. I think you're the strongest of all the girls, Selma. I'm sure you're good at digging.'

'Why can't you get some of the boys to do the digging?'

'Think about it, Selma. I doubt Alistair would be very good at it, but at least he'd be sensible. I wouldn't trust Michael and Peter with spades. They'd start a spade fight in two seconds. Let's see what *you're* like. Maybe I'm wrong. Maybe you won't be able to dig properly.'

'I will.' Selma took her spade. She put her foot on it. She moved a whole chunk of earth. 'See!'

'Yes, I see. Well done! How long can you keep going? There's only five more minutes of playtime, but perhaps we can put in half an hour after lunch . . . Or would that tire you out?'

'I can keep going for ages,' said Selma. 'But am I going to do all the hard work while she just flops about?' She nodded at me and sniffed.

'I'll be doing the hard work too. Tina can carry on collecting up the rubbish, and then tomorrow I'll bring a little trowel so that she can dig up the weeds. I think I might find another big spade just for you, Selma. I'm sure you'll manage it.'

Selma nodded at me triumphantly.

It was very annoying. *I* wanted to be the big strong girl. And I didn't want Selma to have

anything at all to do with my butterfly garden. But I knew I couldn't dig it all. And Miss Lovejoy was an old lady, so I couldn't expect her to dig much either. I had no choice.

Selma went on digging. So did Miss Lovejoy. And I collected litter. Lots and lots of litter.

'I'm going to garden again after lunch,' I told Phil and Maddie while we were eating our sandwiches. (Ham and tomato today. And two cold chipolata sausages, a baby orange called a clementine, two jammy dodgers, and a little bottle of pink lemonade.) I ate everything up. Phil and Maddie looked a bit disappointed.

'Fancy you eating everything,' said Phil.

'Not a crumb left!' said Maddie, peering into my lunch box.

'It's all my hard work gardening.' I yawned and stretched like Dad does when he comes home from work.

'Are you sure you're all right?' Phil asked anxiously. 'You're not meant to do hard work.'

'Mum will be cross. We shouldn't let you do gardening,' said Maddie.

'I like it,' I told them.

'You like being with *Selma*?' said Phil.

'Is she being mean to you?' asked Maddie. 'Shall we come and help too? I don't *have* to play footie.'

I rather wanted them to come. I always felt odd without them, as if two big chunks of me were missing. And we'd get the garden dug much more quickly with two more pairs of hands.

'Yes, come too!' I said eagerly.

But when we went over to the garden patch together, Selma glared at us. Miss Lovejoy didn't look too pleased either.

'What are all you lot doing here?' asked Selma.

'We've come to help with the garden,' said Phil.

'We don't need your help. This is *our* garden.' Selma looked at Miss Lovejoy.

'It's very kind of you to offer your help, Philippa and Madeleine, but I'm afraid I don't have any more spades,' said Miss Lovejoy. 'You go off and play. Tina will be fine. She's chief rubbish collector at the moment.'

'And I'm chief digger. Look!' said Selma, demonstrating.

She dug so fiercely she showered earth all over my socks and shoes. 'Whoops!' she said. Then, 'Sorry, Tina.'

Phil and Maddie looked astonished. Selma Johnson had just apologized to me!!!

'That's OK, Selma,' I said, shaking my feet.

I carried on collecting litter. Selma went on digging. So did Miss Lovejoy. Phil and Maddie wandered off, still looking stunned.

I wished they'd stayed. And yet I felt quite proud too. Miss Lovejoy gave me a big smile.

'You'll never guess what!' said Phil to Mum when she came to collect us after school.

'Our Tina's kind of friends with Selma!' said Maddie.

'We're not friends!' I said. 'But she isn't quite

as mean to me now. We played together at play-time *and* lunch time.'

'Well, that's lovely,' said Mum.

'We do gardening,' I told her proudly.

'Gardening?'

'We're going to make a butterfly garden, Miss Lovejoy says. But it's very hard work, digging and digging.'

'*You're* digging?' said Mum. 'You can't *dig*, Tina! Especially when you've just had pneumonia. Whatever's Miss Lovejoy thinking of!'

'I knew Mum would be cross,' said Maddie.

'I was watching. I don't think Tina did a *lot* of digging,' said Phil.

'She's not to do any digging at all! Do you hear me, Tina? You can't do any gardening,' said Mum.

'But I want to! I *have* to. It's my garden!'

'Well, I'm sorry, but you know you can't do anything that's a strain on your heart.'

'It's not fair!' I said. 'You

don't let me do anything! You're so mean, Mum.'

'Tina! Don't talk to me like that! I know it's not fair, darling, but I can't help it.'

'I want to garden! I want to garden more than anything!' I wailed.

'But you did get ever so out of puff, Tina. I saw you having to lean against the tree,' said Phil.

'*We'll* do the garden and you can watch,' said Maddie.

'I don't want to watch! I'm sick of watching! *I want to garden!*' I yelled.

'Calm down, young lady. I'm not having you throwing a tantrum in the street. Look, we'll go and see Dr Jessop. Maybe she'll be able to talk some sense into you. And I'll get her to write a note to explain the situation to Miss Lovejoy,' said Mum. 'Let's go to her surgery right now.'

Dr Jessop was holding a mother-and-baby clinic.

'This is Dr Jessop's ante-natal afternoon,' said the receptionist. 'I'm afraid you'll have to make an appointment for Tina for tomorrow.'

'Could we wait until Dr Jessop's finished?'

asked Mum. 'I just want a very quick word. It is quite urgent.'

'Very well,' said the receptionist. She's used to Mum and me.

So we sat with all the mothers and babies. There were toddlers who kept running about and grabbing things and shouting. There were crawling babies and crying babies. There were silent babies sucking dummies and squealy babies bouncing on their mother's knee. There were fat babies and thin babies and big babies and very tiny babies. There were babies with curls and babies with wisps and babies with no hair at all.

'Oh, you've got twins!' said one of the mothers. 'So have I – look!'

'Actually, my girls are triplets,' said Mum.

All the mothers looked at Phil and Maddie and me. We hate it when this happens. People always look a bit dismayed when they see me.

Phil didn't mind waiting too much because she actually *likes* babies.

Maddie thinks babies are boring, but she found a football magazine and so she didn't mind waiting too much either.

I looked for a butterfly magazine, but there weren't any. I didn't bother with the babies. I think they're boring too.

I took my sketchbook out of my satchel and looked at all my beautiful butterflies. I read about the flowers they liked to feed on. I ached to make a butterfly garden so that I could watch them fluttering about my very own flowers. I wanted to make it *myself.*

Dr Jessop had to see an awful lot of babies. We all started to get fed up and hungry, so Mum popped out to the newsagent's down the road and came back with a bar of chocolate, which she divided into three.

Phil nibbled her piece daintily. Maddie ate hers in four quick bites. I licked mine like a lolly.

'Oh dear, chocolate!' said the twins' mother. 'I'm never going to give my two chocolates or sweeties. I'll give them raisins or carrot sticks or apple slices if they want a little treat.'

Mum went pink. We're hardly ever allowed chocolate. She scrubbed round my mouth with a tissue, tutting at me.

At long, long last Dr Jessop finished her clinic. She came into the waiting room looking weary.

'Could we just have a very quick word, Dr Jessop?' asked Mum.

Dr Jessop looked even wearier.

'It's Tina,' said Mum.

'Yes, I thought it would be,' said Dr Jessop.

'There's a teacher at her school encouraging her to do gardening – *digging*! Would you please tell Tina that she absolutely mustn't?'

Dr Jessop sat down on one of the waiting-room chairs. 'Why mustn't she?'

Mum looked astonished. 'Well, because of her weak heart – and she's still recovering from that pneumonia. She's as weak as a kitten.'

'Then maybe a bit of fresh air and digging will build her up a bit. We don't want her to play

195

any contact sports because people might barge into her – but gardening sounds like just the ticket.' Dr Jessop looked at me. 'Are you going to grow flowers, Tina, or fruit and vegetables?'

'I'm going to grow everything that butterflies like. It's going to be a butterfly garden,' I said.

'Well, I think that's an excellent idea! I would garden as often as you like – not that there's much you can do over the winter. You can't plant much then.'

'No, but we have to *make* the garden first. It's going to take a long time to do all the digging. Actually, I can't do much of the digging myself, but this girl Selma helps.'

'That's good.' Dr Jessop looked at Phil and Maddie. 'Are you gardening girls too?'

'Well, we wanted to help,' said Phil.

'And I know I'd be good at digging. I bet I'm better than Selma,' said Maddie.

'But it's going to be *my* garden as I'm the one who knows all about butterflies now,' I said proudly.

'Good for you,' said Dr Jessop. 'Well, I'd better be off home to get my family their tea. And I expect you need to do the same, Mrs Maynard . . .'

'Yes. Well. Are you *sure* Tina won't come to any harm doing this gardening? Maddie did say that she was very out of breath and had to lie down . . .'

'No – she just leaned against a tree,' said Maddie.

'It was only a very little lean,' I said.

'I think Tina knows best,' said Dr Jessop. 'If she gets out of puff or tired, then she'll rest. But we need to build up her strength. So you carry on gardening, Tina. If you get a taste for it, you can pop round to my place and earn a bit of pocket money pulling up all *my* weeds.'

So it was decided! Dr Jessop said! I could carry on gardening!

Chapter Fourteen

Selma and I gardened every playtime and every lunch time. Miss Lovejoy gardened with us at first. She was different to the way she was in the classroom. She chatted about all sorts of stuff. She told us about her holidays.

'It's the best part about being a teacher,' she said. 'You get time to go on lovely holidays. I don't spend much during term-time – I don't go out of an evening and I don't bother with fancy new clothes. I save every penny for my holidays.'

She didn't need to tell us that she didn't bother

with fancy new clothes. She had two identical outfits, but in different sludgy colours: a sludgy blue blouse and cardigan and skirt, and a pale sludgy brown blouse and cardigan and skirt.

She always wore the same shoes. I can't wait to wear proper grown-up shoes with high heels. Selma says she's got a pair already, but I think she tells fibs. Miss Lovejoy could wear any style she wanted. Goodness knows why she chose hers!

'Where do you like to go on holiday, Miss Lovejoy?' I asked. 'We went to a caravan in Norfolk. It's lovely there.'

'Yes, it is.'

'Do you go there too?'

'I did when I was a little girl.'

It was very hard to imagine Miss Lovejoy as a little girl.

'Where do you go now?'

'Well, in the long summer holidays I like to explore different countries. I'm planning a trip to Japan next year. I'm trying to learn a little

Japanese, but without much success so far. This last summer I went to Australia.'

'Did you see any kangaroos and koalas?' I asked.

'Only in a zoo. But I was surprised to encounter herds of camels out in the Australian bush. And I desperately wanted to see a Tasmanian devil, but I didn't get lucky. Which was possibly just as well as they're very fierce animals.'

'Do you go away at Christmas and Easter too, Miss Lovejoy?'

'I'm having a little skiing holiday this Christmas. And at Easter I'm planning a long weekend in Paris,' she said dreamily.

Selma and I looked at each other. We tried to imagine Miss Lovejoy skiing and had to bite our lips to stop laughing out loud. This Miss Lovejoy on holiday sounded like a different person altogether.

'Where do you go on holiday, Selma?' I asked.

Selma suddenly went as stiff as her spade. 'All over,' she said quickly.

'Yes, but where?'

'Seaside.'

'In Norfolk?'

'Nah, not boring old Norfolk. We go to Spain and Italy and all them foreign places. Paris.'

'You went to the seaside in Paris?' I said.

'Yeah, so what?'

I knew Selma was fibbing again. I'd been to Paris on a special holiday for poorly children. Mum and Dad and Phil and Maddie had come too. We went to EuroDisney. Paris wasn't anywhere *near* the seaside.

I was about to tell her this triumphantly when I saw Miss Lovejoy frown at me. Frown at me quite fiercely.

So I didn't say anything. I went on digging. I'd cleared up all the horrible litter, and now I was chief uprooter of weeds. Whenever it rained hard overnight and made the earth softer I did a bit of digging too, but only with the little spade.

Later that day, at going-home time, Miss Lovejoy stopped me as I skipped out of the classroom.

'Good girl for holding your tongue about Paris, Tina,' she whispered. 'I could see you were absolutely bursting to say you knew it didn't have a seaside.'

'But why did you want me to keep quiet when you knew Selma was telling fibs?'

'I didn't think it would be tactful to make her look silly. It was all my fault anyway. I should never have started burbling on about holidays.'

I stared at her. Fancy Miss Lovejoy admitting she

was at fault! In class she made out that she was absolutely perfect and always right.

I still didn't understand.

'I don't think Selma ever goes on holidays,' Miss Lovejoy told me.

'What? Not in the summer?' I asked.

'Not ever. Selma's family . . . struggles. She's not a lucky girl like you, Tina.'

I stared. I'd never been called lucky before. I was the scrawny little sick girl, the one who nearly died, the child who wasn't good at lessons, the triplet who was far smaller than her sisters. I was *lucky*?

'Yes, lucky,' Miss Lovejoy repeated. 'You've got lovely sisters who are very kind to you, and a mother who cares so much about you that she comes and beards the old dragon in her den.'

How did Miss Lovejoy *know* Mum called her the old dragon!

I gave a little snigger.

'And I'm sure you have a lovely father who's always very gentle with you,' Miss Lovejoy continued. 'And I know you have a very pretty bedroom and lots of toys and story books. You're allowed to keep pet hamsters. You bring very tasty, nourishing packed lunches to school. You always wear clean, carefully ironed clothes with bright white socks and polished shoes. You've been taught manners and how to speak nicely. You're very lucky, Tina. Think about it.'

She gestured for me to go, and I caught up with Phil and Maddie. I did think about it all the way home. I thought about scary Mrs Johnson who hit Selma. She didn't have a dad – she'd had different stepdads and they all sounded very

fierce. Her whole family looked fierce, even her little brothers.

I didn't know what her bedroom was like, but I couldn't imagine it being pink and white and pretty. I could see for myself that Selma didn't have nice clothes. Her skirt was so old it was shiny at the back and her hem hung down. Her school sweatshirt never got washed at the weekend, so it had stains down the front and grubby sleeves. She didn't have any socks at all, she just wore grubby trainers. They were too tight for her – when she had to take them off for dance and drama there were red marks at her heels and her toes looked sore. And her feet smelled.

Phil and Maddie and I always had a laugh together about Selma's smelly feet, but now it didn't seem quite so funny. I started to feel a bit sorry for Selma, even though she was still the meanest girl ever.

When we were gardening she was still mean to me sometimes, especially when Miss Lovejoy was on playground duty.

'You're still useless at digging, Little Bug,' she said.

'You're so little. My brother Sam's only three, but *he's* bigger than you,' she said.

'You and your sisters think you're so great but you're rubbish. You're all spoiled lah-di-dah babies,' she said.

Each mean thing she said made my stomach clench, as if she'd poked me hard with her spade. Sometimes I nearly cried, but I couldn't because that would make her jeer at me even more.

She never actually poked me with the spade, though sometimes she picked it up and aimed it at me like a machine gun. I knew it was only pretend but I couldn't help squealing all the same.

But then I discovered a marvellous way of getting my own back! *Selma was frightened of worms!*

We hadn't found any worms at all when the earth was still baked hard. But now that it was softer and we could dig deeper, we suddenly came across some.

'Yuck!' said Selma, and she threw her spade down and ran off. '*Worms!*'

'Worms are a wonderful help for gardeners,' said Miss Lovejoy. 'They process the earth for us. It goes in at one end and comes out the other, which makes it much better quality.'

'That's disgusting,' said Selma. 'I'm not digging no more, not if there are worms!'

'*I'm* not frightened of worms. I think they're interesting,' I told her.

'I bet you are frightened!'

'No I'm not. Look!' I bent down and picked up the biggest, wriggliest, pinkest worm and cupped it in my hand.

'Eew!' said Selma, keeping her distance.

I brought my hand up, as if I were going to throw a ball. Selma screamed and ducked.

'Tina!' said Miss Lovejoy. 'Put that worm back in the earth!'

'I wasn't really going to throw it at Selma,' I said. Well, I was considering it, but I didn't think it would be very kind to the worm.

'I should hope not.' Miss Lovejoy was trying to look shocked, but her mouth was twitching as if she wanted to laugh.

Selma went on digging very cautiously. Soon she screamed again.

'Another worm, Selma?' I said. 'Don't worry, I'll sort it. Come on, little wormy. Let's find you another bit of earth, away from that nasty spade. Here, boy. There!'

'You're nuts,' said Selma weakly.

 But now, whenever she started being mean, I just scrabbled in the earth, looking for a worm. She shut up as soon as I found one. Gardening was a lot more peaceful now.

One playtime Harry kicked the football so hard it came bouncing right over to our garden. At that very moment Selma dug up a whole writhing *knot* of worms. She was shrieking her head off.

Harry came running up to get the ball. He stared at Selma. 'What's the matter with her?' he asked me. Then he saw the worms. 'Wow, look at those worms! Is that why you're yelling, Selma? Are you *scared* of worms?'

Selma shut up. She bit her lip.

'She *is* scared, isn't she, Tina?' said Harry, laughing.

I hesitated. I liked Harry so much. I wanted to join in the joke and have a good laugh at Selma with him. It would make me feel really good, wouldn't it?

But when I looked at Selma, I wasn't so sure. 'Oh, Harry!' I said. 'As if Selma would be scared of worms! Selma's not scared of anything.'

'Then why was she yelling her head off?'

'She just stuck her spade right into her foot. *Anyone* would yell,' I said.

'Oh, right.' Harry bounced the ball. 'How come you girls call this a garden? It's just a patch of dirt. Why don't you plant some flowers?'

'We've got to prepare the earth first. It's going to take ages. And then we can't plant most things when it's winter because the ground will be too cold. The roots wouldn't be able to spread out and get all the moisture and goodness,' I said, showing off a bit.

It was weird. I couldn't remember anything Miss Lovejoy said in lessons – but when she talked about gardening I remembered all of it.

Harry started to look bored even though *I* thought I was saying the most interesting things. He ran off back to the football game.

Selma and I went on gardening. She didn't thank me. She didn't say anything at all. She didn't even look at me. But from that day on she stopped being mean to me.

Chapter Fifteen

Selma and I went on digging day after day, week after week.

'You'll have to manage without me for a while, girls,' said Miss Lovejoy. She was walking very stiffly and looked more frowny than usual. 'I've done my back in. It must be all this digging. Maybe it's not such good exercise if you're an old lady!'

'Don't worry, miss,' said Selma. 'Tina and me will do it all.'

'Don't worry, *Miss Lovejoy*,' said Miss Lovejoy. 'But thank you very much, Selma. I know you two girls will carry on valiantly.'

Phil and Maddie were a bit worried about me, the first playtime without Miss Lovejoy. They came and hovered.

'What are you gawping at, Dim Twins?' said Selma. 'Clear off!'

'Don't be like that, Selma,' said Phil. 'We're not getting in the way.'

'We're just watching out for our sister,' said Maddie.

'Well, she's fine. Aren't you, Little Bug?'

'Don't call her that!' said Phil.

'And don't call us Dim Twins either, or we'll start calling *you* names and you won't like it,' said Maddie.

I got worried then. I knew all our private Selma nicknames – Smelly Feet, Snot Face, and worse. I'd once joined in the name-calling at home and we'd all got the most dreadful giggles. But now I didn't want to call Selma names any more. Especially not to her face.

'I'm fine, Phil. I'm fine, Maddie. You go now.'

I said it so fiercely that they wandered off, looking slightly hurt. They still checked up on me every now and then. Some of the other children came to see what we were doing too.

'Can *I* do some digging, Selma?' asked Kayleigh.

It looked like she'd got fed up with her dancing. She was still Selma's sort of friend in class. I was worried. Selma on her own was starting to be OK, but Selma and Kayleigh together might well gang up on me.

'Go on, Selma. Give us a spade,' said Kayleigh.

Oh dear. We did have a spare spade. Selma was using the big spade now – 'Because I know I can trust you to be very careful with it,' Miss Lovejoy had said. So we had one smaller spade that wasn't being used.

Selma looked at it. And then she looked at me. 'Sorry, Kayleigh,' she said. 'This is our private garden. Only us two can dig in it.'

'*She's* not digging,' said Kayleigh, nodding at me.

She was right. I was having a little rest, picking out some big stones and re-homing worms instead.

'She's not strong enough to dig dig dig all the time. Not like me. But she's still doing garden work,' said Selma. 'Now clear off and do your stupid dancing, Kayleigh.'

Kayleigh did clear off. But then Peter and Mick came ambling over.

'Want us to do some gardening, you two?' asked Peter.

'We've got muscles – look.' Mick posed to show off his arms. 'We're big and strong as gorillas!' He thumped his chest and made mad gorilla noises.

I couldn't help giggling.

Selma gave me a look. 'Don't encourage them,' she said. 'Clear off, you boys. This is our garden, me and Tina's.'

Alistair was even less welcome. He didn't offer to dig. He wouldn't have been any better at it than me. He offered advice instead.

'How many weeks have you been digging now? And you're not even halfway finished. You do realize, if you'd got the whole class to dig this patch, then you'd have done it all long ago.'

'But there wouldn't be any point, Mr Smarty-Pants, because we're not going to start planting until spring next year,' said Selma.

'And then all the butterflies will come,' I said, seeing huge flocks of butterflies swooping over the playground and landing on our garden like a fluttering mosaic.

'Not necessarily,' said Alistair, in his loud booming voice. 'There aren't any caterpillars around here, are there? I think it's going to take several seasons for your butterfly garden to work properly.'

'It will *so* work,' I said, wanting to kick him.

'And I doubt you're going to get plants to grow in this earth anyway,' he went on.

'Yes we will. It's ever so wormy,' said Selma.

'But it doesn't look right,' said Alistair, bending down to

inspect it. 'I'm one hundred per cent certain you need some kind of compost. That's what my father uses in *his* garden.'

'I'm one hundred per cent certain I'm going to whack you with my spade if you don't clear off,' said Selma.

We looked at each other when he was gone.

'What's compost?' I asked.

'Haven't got a clue,' said Selma. 'Oh, that Alistair! He really does my head in!'

'Me too,' I said. But I was starting to worry. Alistair was nearly always one hundred per cent right.

I was in trouble with Miss Lovejoy that afternoon because my spelling was even worse than usual.

I carnt do speling rite

'You *can* spell when you want to, Tina. You can spell chrysalis and buddleia and antennae, and they're very difficult words. You're very exasperating,' said Miss Lovejoy.

'Yes, Miss Lovejoy.' I wondered if she'd finished telling me off. 'Miss Lovejoy, what's compost?'

'Can we concentrate on your spelling just now, Tina?'

'Yes, Miss Lovejoy. But when we're finished, will you tell me what compost is, because Alistair says plants won't grow without it.'

'Alistair is right,' she said. 'As always.' She sounded as if he irritated her a little bit too. 'I have a compost heap at home in my garden. It's all my vegetable peelings and rotted down leaves. I rake it into the soil and it makes it richer.'

'Can you spare some for the butterfly garden?'

'There wouldn't be anywhere near enough. We'll need to buy several bags of compost from a garden centre.'

'Oh. So you have to pay for it?'

'I'm afraid so.'

'Do you think you can buy compost from a pound shop?'

'I think big bags of compost cost a lot more than a pound.'

I sighed heavily. I had precisely fifty pence in

my piggy bank. I could save up my pocket money – though it would be awful watching Phil and Maddie buy sweets and necklaces and rings and tiny animals and comics and treats for Nibbles and Speedy and Cheesepuff if *I* had to save every penny.

Still, it would be worth it to get a butterfly garden. Then I had another realization. I hit myself on the side of my head. 'Oh no!' I groaned.

'What's the matter, Tina? Are you overcome with shame because of your atrocious spelling?' asked Miss Lovejoy.

'No, I just thought of something else. Do plants cost money too?'

'I'm afraid they do.'

'Even weedy plants like nettles?'

'Well, I dare say you could help yourself to some nettles growing wild and no one would mind. But you will need to buy shrubs and seedlings from a garden centre.'

'They're going to cost a lot, aren't they?'

'Yes, I'm afraid so. You're going to need lots and lots of plants if you want to attract all the butterflies in the neighbourhood. Fifty pounds' worth. Maybe even a hundred.'

A hundred pounds! I'd never had that much money in my life. Only grown-ups had that sort of money.

I took a deep breath. 'You couldn't possibly help a bit with funding, could you, Miss Lovejoy? Seeing as it's your butterfly garden as well as Selma's and mine?'

'My goodness, you've got a cheek, young lady!' said Miss Lovejoy, though she looked amused rather than cross. 'Still, if you don't ask you don't get. Although I'm afraid you won't get anything at all from me. I save every penny for my holidays, you know that. But I'm happy to make a suggestion. Why don't you and Selma try to raise funds?'

'How can we do that?'

'You could have a sale at school – maybe make cakes and biscuits to sell at playtime . . . And we always have a Christmas fete in December.

I could let you and Selma have a special white elephant stall, if you like.'

'A white elephant stall?' I said, baffled.

'It's a stall where you can buy anything, old or new – rare items, like white elephants.'

'Like a junk stall?'

'More or less. And perhaps you could get people to sponsor you on a walk?'

'But I can't walk very far, so I wouldn't raise much.'

'I tell you what – I'll sponsor you in a spelling test. I'll make you a list of all the words you have difficulty with – and we both know there are a great many! Then I'll give you time to learn them, and if you get them all right – *nearly* all right – I'll contribute some money for plants.'

I stared at her.

That was a *very* crafty suggestion! I hoped it would be a *lot* of money.

The last lesson was art. Miss Lovejoy showed us a painting of people in a park – when you looked closely, you could see that they were all made of little coloured dots.

Then we had to do our own dotty pictures.

'I bet you do a butterfly, Little Bug,' said Selma. She still called me that, but it was just a habit now.

'You bet wrong, Big Bug,' I said. 'I'm going to draw a dotty sponge cake. And dotty cupcakes. And dotty chocolate brownies. And dotty cookies. And dotty flapjacks.'

'Are you extra hungry or something?'

'No, I'm making plans. We're going to have a cake sale to raise money for compost and plants. Are you any good at making cakes, Selma?'

'Don't know. Never tried,' she said.

'I made a cake out of a packet once. Phil and Maddie and me did. And we get to stir the mixture when Mum makes cupcakes. And lick out the bowl – that's the best bit. Let's make lots and lots of cakes and cookies,' I said.

'Where are we going to make them?'

'At home,' I said. 'I'll make some and you make some too.'

Selma hesitated. 'Can't be bothered,' she said.

'Oh go on, Selma! I can't make enough for everyone, even with Phil and Maddie helping,' I said.

'Tough,' said Selma, and she wouldn't talk to me any more, even though I kept leaning across Alistair to try to persuade her.

'If you don't mind my saying, it's extremely annoying having a person talking right through me,' he said. 'And you keep jogging me, Tina, and turning my dots into splodges. But I'll make you a date and walnut loaf for your cake sale. Daddy and I often make one. As a matter of fact, Mummy says my date loaves are better than Daddy's. She says she's one hundred per cent certain of it.'

'We don't need you to do your weirdo date loaves,' said Selma rudely. 'This cake sale is just for Tina and me.'

'But I thought you didn't want to be bothered, Selma,' I said. 'And we need all the cakes we can get. Thank you very much, Alistair. We'd love to have one of your date and walnut loaves.'

I wasn't so sure about that. I'd seen Alistair eating buttered slices of his date and walnut loaf at lunch time and it looked very dark and treacly, but I didn't want to hurt his feelings. 'I like walnuts,' I said politely.

'On second thoughts, maybe I'll leave out the walnuts, because some children have nut allergies,' said Alistair.

'That's very thoughtful of you, Alistair,' I managed to say.

I looked at Selma. 'Are you sure you won't even make *one* cake, Selma? What about chocolate crispy cakes – they're ever so easy-peasy.'

'I'm not messing around making stupid cakes,' she said. 'Now shut up about it.'

So I did.

When we were going home, I told Mum and Phil and Maddie all about Miss Lovejoy's cake sale suggestion.

'I can make some cakes, can't I, Mum?' I asked.

'Of course.'

'And do you want us to make cakes too? Or is this just for you and Selma?' asked Phil.

'Your new bestie Selma?' Maddie mocked.

'Selma isn't my best friend, silly! And of course I want you to make the cakes too,' I said, giving Maddie and Phil a poke. 'Especially as Selma can't be bothered – which I think is very mean of her. She's weird. She can be almost nice, especially when we're digging in our garden, but then she suddenly goes back to being mean. And imagine not wanting to make cakes when it's such fun, especially when you can lick out the bowl afterwards.'

'Maybe Selma never makes cakes at home,'

said Mum. 'Tell you what – would you like to invite her to tea, Tina, and then she can make cakes with you? What about this Thursday? Then you could have your cake sale on Friday.'

'Mum! Have you gone crazy!' said Phil.

'We don't want Selma Johnson to come to tea! She's still our worst enemy,' said Maddie.

'I wasn't asking you two, I was asking Tina,' said Mum. '*Would* you like Selma to come to tea, Tina?'

I thought about it for a few seconds, walking with one foot in the gutter and one on the pavement to help me concentrate.

Selma wasn't really my worst enemy any more, even though she certainly wasn't my best friend. But I wasn't at all sure about inviting her to tea. What if she came into our bedroom? She'd tease terribly about our china dolls. That made me think about Baby and all the old pain came back.

'No, of course I don't want Selma to come to tea! No one ever, ever, ever asks *Selma* to tea,' I said.

'Then maybe that's all the more reason to invite her,' said Mum. 'I think it would be a good idea, Tina.'

I started wavering.

'That's not really fair, Mum,' said Phil. 'Why can Tina have Selma to tea – I kept asking if I could have Neera and all our club to tea and you said you were too busy.'

'All right, you ask Neera to tea on Thursday. I'm sure she'd like to make cakes too. But not all those other girls or it'll turn into a proper party and I really *am* too busy for that.'

'It's not fair if Phil and Tina have people to tea and I can't,' said Maddie.

'You can. Who would you like to invite?' Mum asked.

'Harry!'

'You can't ask *Harry*!' said Phil. 'This is going to be a girls' cake-making party.'

'It's *not* a party,' said Mum. 'And Maddie can invite Harry if she likes.'

'Boys don't make cakes,' said Phil.

'They do, actually,' I said. 'Alistair is going to make me a date loaf for my cake stall.'

'Look, if you invite Alistair too, I'll *know* you've gone nuts,' said Phil.

'Not nuts. Alistair is leaving the walnuts out of his date loaf in case some children have nut allergies,' I said. 'And I'm not inviting Alistair because he'd boss us about and tell us we weren't doing it properly.'

'But you think you'd like to invite Selma?' Mum asked.

'Maybe,' I said. 'Let me think about it a bit more.'

Chapter Sixteen

I invited Selma to tea. Her face screwed up, and I thought at first that she was going to say something really horrid, maybe even hit me. Then I wondered if she might be going to cry – though of course that was silly. Selma never ever cried. She just made other people cry.

'Can you come? I know you don't really like making cakes, but perhaps we could make some together so we can have a cake sale on Friday. I'll let *you* lick out the bowl,' I said, making a supremely generous offer.

Selma didn't thank me. She didn't say I was

very kind. She didn't say anything at all. She just shrugged her shoulders and nodded.

Phil invited Neera to tea. Neera squealed and threw her arms round Phil.

Maddie invited Harry to tea. He said, 'Yay!' and did keepy-uppies with his football.

Selma didn't look too happy to hear that Neera and Harry were coming. 'I thought it was going to be just us,' she said, frowning.

'Yes, but Phil invited Neera because she's her friend. And Maddie invited Harry because he's her friend. And I invited you,' I said.

'Because I'm your friend?' asked Selma.

'Well. Sort of,' I said, wondering if she'd object.

But weirdly she didn't object at all. She smiled.

For once we didn't do gardening at playtime and lunch time. We made a poster about our Friday cake sale instead. I drew lots of cakes and buns and cookies, properly this time, not with funny little dots. Selma coloured part of it in, and I let her do the lettering too. She went over the lines a bit and her printing went sideways, but it didn't really matter.

Miss Lovejoy let us pin it up on the big notice board by the school entrance.

I was still rather worried about tea and the cake-making session. We were such a weird mixture. I thought Neera might want to go off with Phil and do their club stuff together. I thought Harry might want to mess about and play footie indoors. I thought Selma might try to boss everyone about and be mean.

It was strange coming home from school, the three of us with Selma and Neera and Harry. We were a bit of a squash on the pavement.

When we got home, Gran and Grandad were there!

'We're going to have three cake-making teams,' said Mum. 'I'm going to have Phil and Neera in my team. Gran's going to have Maddie and Harry in her team. And Grandad's having Tina and Selma in *his* team. Then, when the girls' dad gets home from work, he can be the chief judge and decide which team has made the best cakes.'

'Just like *The Great British Bake Off,*' said Neera. 'I love that programme!'

'First of all you'd better rush straight upstairs and wash your hands really well. Then we'll have a snack to keep us going. And then it's *Ready, Steady, Bake!*' said Mum.

We had banana sandwiches and hot chocolate with a marshmallow floating on the frothy cream.

'I love the way you do hot chocolate, Mrs Maynard,' said Harry.

'Yes, it's truly yummy,' said Neera.

Selma didn't say anything, but she drank her hot chocolate right down to the last drop and had three helpings of banana sandwiches.

'I like a girl with an appetite,' said Grandad. 'I'm glad you're in my team, Selma.'

Team 1

Team 2

Team 3

Mum had laid out the kitchen table very carefully. She'd borrowed extra scales and basins and jugs from Gran and Mrs Richards next door. Phil and Maddie and I already had our own aprons, but Mum had made three more out of old dish towels and tape. These were for Selma and Neera and Harry.

Mum wore her pretty flowery apron, Gran wore a frilly check apron, and Grandad wore a very rude apron.

'Grandad!' said Phil, very embarrassed, but Maddie and Neera and Harry and Selma and I all laughed, especially when Grandad did a little dance.

'He's a right laugh, your grandad,' said Selma.

So then we all set about baking. We measured and mixed and stirred and rolled and filled all the tins and pans, and then we put our first batch in the oven. While the cakes were cooking, we measured and mixed and stirred and rolled and filled more tins and pans, ready to go into the oven as soon as the first batch was done. Then, when the first batch had cooled, we spread the sponges with jam and cream, and decorated all the cakes with icing and silver balls and rainbow sprinkles. While we waited for the second batch to cook, we licked out the bowls (the best bit of all!).

Then we did the washing-up while Mum and Gran made spaghetti bolognese for tea and Grandad had a beer, because he said baking was thirsty work. Dad came home just in time for the spaghetti.

'Don't eat too much of it!' said Mum. 'You've got lots of cake sampling to do afterwards.'

'I want to eat lots!' said Harry. 'Spag bol's my absolute favourite.'

'Mine too,' said Neera.

'Don't you have Indian food at home?' Gran asked her.

'Yes, but when we eat out we go to the Italian restaurant.'

'Do you like spaghetti, Selma?' asked Grandad.

Selma was looking rather worried. 'It's a bit . . . wormy,' she said.

'Haven't you ever had spaghetti before?' said Maddie.

'Yeah, course I have,' said Selma. She stuck her fork into her spaghetti. She didn't know how to wind it up – she munched and slurped and got sauce all over herself.

'Oh, Selma, you're making an awful mess!' said Phil.

'No, she's eating it the way *I* like to eat spaghetti – with enthusiasm!' said Grandad. 'You're a girl after my own heart, Selma.' He munched and slurped and got sauce all over his face as well.

Harry roared with laughter and copied him. So I did too. It was great fun.

Mum frowned, but she couldn't really tell me off or she'd have to tell Selma and Harry and Grandad off too.

'Right, we'd better wash our mucky faces,' said Grandad when we'd finished. 'Come here, young Selma. My goodness, you've got sauce right round your ears!'

He scrubbed at her with a clean J-cloth while she wriggled and giggled. When we were all clean, we led Dad to the worktop where all our cakes were on display. Mum and Phil and Neera had made cupcakes and a jam and cream sponge. Gran and Maddie and Harry had made fairy cakes and a lemon drizzle cake. Grandad and Selma and I had made butterfly cakes and a chocolate cake.

I especially liked our butterfly cakes, even though they didn't look like *real* butterflies.

'My goodness me, how can I possibly judge?' said Dad. 'They all look so splendid.'

He could only judge the sponge and lemon drizzle and chocolate cake by their appearance, because it would spoil them to cut into them.

'But I can sample a cupcake and a fairy cake and a butterfly cake!' he said.

He ate a mouthful of each, going 'Mmmm, yummy, absolutely delicious,' each time.

'Well, Dad?'

'Which do you like best?'

'Is it the butterfly cake?'

'I'll have to have another bite to make up my mind,' said Dad.

He had another careful munch of all three.

'Do you know, it's almost impossible to choose. So I declare . . . all three teams number one winners!'

So we all got a prize – a tiny teddy wearing a chef's hat and a T-shirt with NUMBER ONE CHEF on it.

There were only six teddies, so Mum and Gran and Grandad didn't get one, but they didn't seem to mind.

'We'll have a prize drink instead,' said Grandad.

Phil and Neera and Maddie and Harry and Selma and me all tried a crumb of each cake. I secretly thought the butterfly cakes were by far the best. Selma thought so too. But we just whispered it to each other.

Neera's dad came to take her home.

Then Harry's big brother came to take him home.

No one came to take Selma home for ages and ages. We didn't mind. I showed her my butterfly book. I'd added lots more butterflies to it now. I was a bit worried she might turn back into Mean Selma and say nasty things or even scribble on the pages, but she just looked at all the pictures and read the words.

'So we've definitely got to plant this buddleia in our garden,' she said.

'Yep. Let's make a list of all the plants that British butterflies like.'

We made a long list, and I added fruit too, though I wasn't sure we could wait for an apple tree to grow, and I knew it wasn't warm enough to grow an orange tree unless we had a proper greenhouse.

'Even so, we'll need lots of cake sales to afford this lot,' I said. 'But Miss Lovejoy says we can have a stall at the Christmas fete. And I've got to do this rubbish sponsored spelling test!'

'I'll help you with your spellings,' said Selma.

Her spelling was only a little bit better than mine. Maddie looked as if she was about to point this out, but I glared at her.

It got to way past our bedtime, and still no one came for Selma.

'Tell you what – we can run young Selma home in our car,' said Grandad. 'We'll have to be setting off soon.'

'Oh yeah, please!' said Selma. She liked my grandad.

But then there was a knock at the door, and it was Selma's mum at last.

'Sorry. Got held up. You know how it is,' she said. She looked as if she'd been to a party.

'Come on, Selma. You been making these cakes then?' she asked.

249

'Here, Selma, I'll pop a couple of your butterfly cakes in a bag and you can take them home with you,' said Mum.

I felt a bit irritated. The cakes weren't supposed to be given away!

'Oh, they look fancy!' said Mrs Johnson. 'You never made them yourself, Selma!'

'She did. More or less. She's an excellent little baker, your daughter,' said Grandad.

Selma gave him a big grin.

'Say thank you nicely to everyone then,' Mrs Johnson told her.

Selma mumbled something, and then did the most extraordinary thing. She put her arms round me and gave me a big hug!

Phil and Maddie didn't half tease me afterwards when we were in bed.

'She *is* your best friend now!' said Phil.

'Fancy having Selma Johnson for a best friend!' said Maddie.

'She's *not* a best friend. *You're* my best friends,' I said. 'Selma's just a *friend* friend. Sometimes. When she's not being mean.'

'Aren't you still a bit scared of her?' Phil asked.

'You would tell us if she was still being horrid?' Maddie asked.

I thought hard about it. 'I don't *think* I'm scared now. And she isn't really horrid any more. Well, she's still a bit bossy with me, but I don't mind.'

Selma's bossiness came in very useful at the cake sale.

Miss Lovejoy let us set out all the cakes on paper plates ten minutes before the bell went for playtime. We cut the big cakes into neat slices and displayed the cupcakes and fairy cakes and butterfly cakes in pretty patterns.

We cut Alistair's date loaf into squares. There was no way we could make it look pretty, but I suppose it did look very healthy.

We decided to charge 50p per cake, to make it easy to do the adding up and giving change. Miss Lovejoy gave us an old Quality Street tin to keep the money in.

We weren't prepared for the rush the minute the bell went. It wasn't just our class. Lots of other children crammed themselves into our classroom – even some of the Year Sixes. And the teachers all came too! We had so many people barging into our table and asking for cakes and waving their money that it almost got scary.

'Stop pushing, everyone!' Selma yelled. 'Form a proper queue! No shoving, no mucking about or I'll thump you one!' She sounded so fierce that even the big Year Sixes stopped pushing and waited meekly.

Miss Lovejoy had a little word with Mrs Brownlow, the head teacher, and we had ten minutes longer at playtime, so we could sell all our cakes. Alistair bought three slices of his own date loaf. Nobody else bought it until Miss Simpson, our music teacher, saw it.

There was just one butterfly cake left that had got a bit bashed. Selma and I shared it. It still tasted good.

Miss Lovejoy let us count up our fifty pences during our maths lesson. We'd made £32.50!

'Wow, that's a fortune!' I said. 'That's enough for at least two bags of compost.'

'Yeah, but haven't we got to pay your mum for all the flour and sugar and butter and stuff we used to make the cakes?' asked Selma. 'My mum said they must have cost a bomb. She said your mum must have more money than sense. She thinks she's stupid.'

'Oh,' I said, taken aback.

'But *I* think your mum's nice. And I *love* your grandad. You're so lucky. I haven't got a grandad.'

'Well, maybe you can have a share of mine, because he likes you too,' I said.

I was still worrying about Mum. I didn't like her being insulted. And I hadn't even thought about how much the ingredients must have cost.

'Perhaps we ought to give my mum . . . half our profits from the cake sale?' I said.

'It's up to you. You're the one in charge of the money,' said Selma.

I'd offered to share it out but Selma shook her head.

'Don't be mad. I'm not taking any of that money home. Someone would nick it straight away. My stepdad would be down the pub or the betting shop with it.'

'Even if you explained that it was our money and we're saving it for compost and plants?'

'Yep. Wouldn't make any difference. They'd say I was soft in the head anyway, spending it on muck and weeds.'

'But it's for a butterfly garden!' I said.

'Yeah, but my mum and them don't reckon butterflies the way you do. They just think they're silly bugs and try to swat them.'

'You reckon butterflies though, don't you, Selma?'

'Not quite as much as you – but yeah, they're OK. And I want to make this garden. Imagine if I've done all this digging for nothing!'

'You've been a champion digger, Selma,' I said, and I clapped her on the back.

I *did* offer Mum half the cake money as I proudly carried the heavy Quality Street tin home.

'Oh, that's sweet of you, Tina,' she said.

'Well, it was actually Selma's idea, not mine,' I admitted.

'My goodness. Selma's quite a thoughtful girl when she wants to be,' said Mum. 'But anyway, you two keep the money for your garden. Dad got a discount on all the cake ingredients because he bought them from his supermarket. And we were happy to let you have a little party. It was good fun – wasn't it, Phil and Maddie?'

'Yes, it was quite good fun,' said Phil. 'But I think it would only be fair for *me* to have a cake-making party with Neera so we can buy stuff for our club.'

'And *I* want a cake-making party with Harry so we can buy cool new football stuff,' said Maddie.

'You girls!' said Mum. '*I* want a cake-making party with all my friends so I can buy some new clothes! Now quit nagging me. At least Tina's cake sale was a big success and she can buy stuff for her butterfly garden.'

Phil gave a big yawn. 'I'm actually getting a bit fed up with hearing about this boring old butterfly garden.'

'Me too,' said Maddie. 'And I'm especially fed up with everyone praising yucky old Selma all the time. She mightn't be quite so mean now, but she's still pretty horrible. I don't get you, Tina. There you are, being all best friendies with her now, when she was the girl who flushed your Baby down the toilet!'

'I keep *saying*, she's not my best friend. You shut up!' I said.

'No, *you* shut up,' said Maddie.

'Don't say *shut up*, say *be quiet*,' said Mum. 'And all three of you, be quiet!'

We squabbled most of the evening. It was awful, because we don't usually fight. Phil and Maddie didn't even say goodnight to me properly when we went to bed.

I pretended I didn't care, but I did. I couldn't get to sleep. I lay on my tummy with my head under my pillow, thinking about Baby and missing her badly.

Then Phil pattered across the carpet and climbed into my bed. 'Sorry, Tina! I don't really think butterfly gardens are boring,' she whispered.

Maddie came and climbed into my bed on the other side. 'Sorry, Tina! I won't go on about Selma any more, even though I still can't stand her,' she said.

It was a bit of a squash, but I didn't mind a bit. We cuddled up close and went to sleep together, Phil and Maddie and me.

Chapter Seventeen

We started to collect things for our white elephant stall at the Christmas fete.

'What sort of things?' asked Selma.

'We'll make stuff. And we'll collect up old stuff and sell that too,' I said.

'I can't make stuff. And I haven't *got* any old stuff,' she said.

Miss Lovejoy overheard. 'It will be my pleasure to teach you to make something, girls,' she said.

The next day she came into our classroom carrying some thick cream material, little skeins of different coloured wool, and two big thick needles.

'Cross-stitch purses!' she said.

Oh, those purses! At first they made us *very* cross as we stitched.

But we slowly got better at it. We couldn't always dig because it was too cold or too wet, so we sat and stitched instead.

Selma made a rainbow purse. It was a little bit wobbly, but she did the colours in the right order and it looked very pretty.

'What's that yellow blobby thing on the ground?' I asked.

'It's the crock of gold. You get that at the end of the rainbow,' she told me.

I made a butterfly purse. *Two* butterfly purses. I made a blue morpho butterfly purse and an emerald swallowtail purse. I knew two girls who might want to buy them!

Miss Lovejoy lined the purses and stitched up the sides for us, but we sewed on the big press studs.

I drew butterfly pictures too – little ones

on good white paper – colouring them in very carefully. Miss Lovejoy let us have some pink and blue card from the store cupboard. Selma cut it into rectangles, measuring very carefully so the sides didn't go wonky. She stuck my butterfly pictures on them and little calendar booklets underneath. Miss Lovejoy provided the calendar booklets too.

Phil and Neera made necklaces and bracelets for our stall.

Maddie and Harry tried to make plasticine footballers, but they went all lumpy so they squashed them up again. They donated some old things instead. Maddie gave a few books and a pretend make-up set and her rabbit with the silly face. Harry gave a ball and an old football strip. Kayleigh donated some dance DVDs. She didn't want to donate any-thing at all, but Selma said she must, because she was on our table and had to support us.

Peter donated a small box of Lego. He admitted it probably had a few pieces missing.

 Mick donated a Jolly Octopus game. Selma and I played it with him before we put it in the store cupboard for our stall.

Alistair donated a dark brown cake.

'Oh, Alistair, not *another* date loaf,' Selma groaned. 'There are only two people in the whole world who like your date loaf. You and weirdo Miss Simpson.'

'That's not one hundred per cent accurate,' he said. 'My mum likes my date loaf – well, she likes the version with nuts in. And so does my dad. And anyway, this *isn't* a date loaf. It's an organic healthy version of a Christmas cake.'

'Where's the Icing and that yellow stuff?' asked Selma.

'Marzipan ... I said this is a *healthy* version that won't rot your teeth. And it's got excellent keeping qualities, especially if you put it in a tin.'

'It's very kind of you, Alistair, but the thing

is, we weren't really going to have another cake stall,' I said, trying to be more tactful. 'We're not having anything you can eat. We're going to sell all sorts of things, old and new. It's a white elephant stall. That means—'

'I know what it means!' said Alistair. 'All right, I'll take my cake back. I can always give it to my auntie for Christmas. I'll bring you something highly appropriate for your white elephant stall tomorrow.'

Selma and I had a private laugh, imagining all the things Alistair might bring from home.

But Alistair brought us a wonderful gift for our stall.

'Oh, Alistair, it's magnificent!' I said.

'What are you giving this away for?' asked Selma. 'Most people give old junky stuff. This elephant looks brand-new and expensive.'

'I've had it ever since I was little, but I'm always very careful with my possessions,' said Alistair. 'He's called Ganesh after the Indian god.'

'Well, we'll re-christen him Alistair, after you, and we'll put him in pride of place on our stall. Thank you very much!' I said.

Mum donated some real make-up and a perfume-and-hand-lotion set, still in its box, and some artificial flowers.

Dad donated his new cardigan. Mum got cross because she'd only just bought it for him, replacing the old stripy jumper he's had for years and years. Dad said he hated wearing his new cardigan because it made him feel like an old man and there was nothing wrong with his stripy jumper.

I phoned Gran and Grandad, and they sent a big parcel full of things for the butterfly garden stall.

Gran donated some scarves and shoes and handbags.

Grandad donated some books and DVDs.

Selma's family donated some things

too. She came into class with all sorts stuffed into her school bag. 'Look what I got,' she said, showing me proudly.

'Oh, Selma, how kind of your family to donate these,' I said.

'Well, they didn't exactly *realize* they were donating,' she said, grinning.

I looked at her anxiously. 'Won't you get into trouble when they find they're missing?'

'Oh, stuff always goes missing in our house. And I'm always in trouble anyway,' said Selma, shrugging.

So one way or another we had HEAPS to sell on our butterfly stall. I spent ages trying to price them appropriately.

On the Saturday of the sale we got to school very early to set up our stall. Phil and Maddie were with me, so they helped. They had to do it the way Selma and I wanted, because it was our stall after all. It was great fun bossing them about!

Miss Lovejoy was at school early too. She brought some little boxes with her. 'Here you are, girls. I thought you might like to sell these on your white elephant stall,' she said.

She'd made the most beautiful little butterfly brooches, with painted wings and embroidered markings and bodies, and a pin at the back.

'Oh, Miss Lovejoy, they're simply wonderful!' I said.

I was so thrilled, I forgot that she was scary Miss Lovejoy, my teacher. I rushed up and gave her a big hug.

'Now now, no need to be quite so enthusiastic, Tina!' she said, backing away, but she looked pleased all the same.

'I want one of the butterfly brooches,' I said, examining them all.

'So do I,' said Selma. 'Tell you what, price them very, very cheaply and then we'll both be able to afford one.'

'Yes, but they're so lovely we should really ask

a lot for them so that we make masses of money,' I said.

'Perhaps we could price just two of them very cheaply . . .' said Selma. 'One for me and one for you.'

'That would be cheating,' I told her firmly.

'Oh, you're such a goody-goody, Little Bug. You make me sick at times,' said Selma.

'You make *me* sick too, Big Bug,' I said, and I mimed being sick all over her.

Then she pretended to be sick on me, and I pretended to be sick on her and—

'Stop it! You're being disgusting!' said Phil.

'Utterly gross!' agreed Maddie, but she was giggling.

We decided to charge five pounds each for the butterfly brooches because they were so very special.

We sold three of them even before the Christmas fete was officially opened by some local lady writer.

The lady writer bought one of the butterfly brooches too. She wanted the blue morpho butterfly purse as well, but I had to tell her that it was reserved for my sister.

Phil did want it, and Maddie wanted the emerald swallowtail purse, just as I'd hoped.

We were very, very busy selling things on our stall. The other butterfly brooches sold in the first half-hour.

'I *did* want one,' said Selma. 'We're daft not to have kept two for ourselves.'

'But look at all the money we've made!' I shook the Quality Street tin.

Mum came and bought Dad's cardigan back! 'It's a lovely colour and very thick wool. If your dad won't wear it, I'll give it to Grandad,' she said.

Selma's mum came too, with her little brothers.

'Are you behaving yourself then, our Selma?' she asked.

'Course I am,' said Selma. 'Are you going to buy something from our stall, Mum?'

'It's just a load of old tat,' said Mrs Johnson rudely. But then she saw the packet of tights. She picked them up and peered at them. 'I love this make – and they're my size!' she said. 'I'll have them.'

Selma took the money happily. I didn't dare look at her in case we both burst out laughing.

We were making *lots* of money. We even sold Alistair's white elephant, though at ten pounds, it was the most expensive item on our stall (Miss Simpson bought it!).

When we only had a few items left to sell, Selma and I left Phil and Maddie in charge of the stall so we could wander around and see what else was happening at the fete.

There were sweet stalls and toy stalls and hand-knitted jumper stalls and book stalls and pottery stalls and a roll-a-penny stall and a tombola, and Father Christmas sat up on the stage with a big sack full of wrapped presents. Not the real Father Christmas, of course. It was someone dressed up.

'It *isn't*!' said Selma.

'It *is*!' I said. 'It's fifty p a go. Come on – Mum's given me a pound to spend. Let's go and see him!'

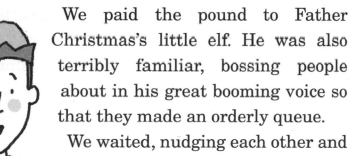

We paid the pound to Father Christmas's little elf. He was also terribly familiar, bossing people about in his great booming voice so that they made an orderly queue.

We waited, nudging each other and giggling.

'Hello, Father Christmas!' said Selma when we got to the front. 'My, what a big tummy you've got! You must have been eating loads of mince pies.'

'I would mind your manners, little girl,' said Father Christmas in a very familiar voice. He frowned at Selma, his beady eyes very bright. 'If you don't behave yourself, you won't get a present!'

'But I've paid my fifty p, Father Christmas. At least, my friend Tina here has paid for me,' she said.

'Then you *and* your friend will go without unless you're very humble and polite and well-mannered.'

'We'll be extra specially humble and polite and well-mannered, Father Christmas,' I said quickly, adding, 'We've got a very strict teacher who always tries to get us to mind our manners.'

'Ho ho ho!' said Father Christmas. 'Come along then, little girls. Have a quick delve in my sack for a present.'

Selma dived in first and brought out the biggest parcel she could find. I copied her, going for the next biggest parcel.

'Mmm. If *I* were you, I'd go for something quite little. And squarish. And as my costume is bright tomato red, perhaps that's a hint about my favourite colour. I've probably wrapped the very best presents in a similar shade. Why don't you pop those presents back and try again.'

So that's exactly what we did. I'm better at

delving than Selma. I went right to the bottom of the sack and felt around until I found two small parcels. I brought them out into daylight and found that they were both wrapped in bright red paper.

'Please may we have these ones, Father Christmas?' I asked excitedly.

'Ho ho ho. Excellent choices!' said Father Christmas.

We tore the wrappings off straight away. Can you guess what they were?

Chapter Eighteen

On the last day of term I gave Miss Lovejoy a special Christmas present. I'd agonized for a long time over what to get her. She'd been very kind to me, and she'd given me my special colouring pencils and the butterfly book. She'd made sure that Selma and I got a butterfly brooch too. I wanted to give her something splendid – but I also wanted to save every penny of my pocket money for the butterfly garden.

'Why don't you draw Miss Lovejoy a picture?' Phil suggested.

'I've already given her a butterfly picture,' I said.

'Draw something else then,' said Maddie. 'Fuss fuss fuss over boring old Miss Lovejoy! You're such a teacher's pet now, Tina!'

'Well, she's nice to me. I want to show her I'm grateful,' I said.

'I'll buy a bottle of wine or a big box of chocolates,' said Mum. 'It can be a present from all three of you.'

'Yes, but I want to give her my *own* present too,' I said.

I thought and thought and thought. What would Miss Lovejoy really, really like? She'd said herself that she didn't like to spend money on clothes or fancy meals. She liked to save up for her holidays. I remembered she was hoping to go to Japan next summer. Aha!

On the way home from school Mum often took us to the library. This time I didn't choose story books. I found a book about Japan instead. Then I spent the entire evening drawing Miss Lovejoy a picture of Japan. I bolted my tea down in ten minutes and

didn't watch any television at all. I just drew and coloured as carefully as I could.

I copied great tall skyscraper buildings and ancient old temples and pagodas and strange little teahouses with hardly any furniture and a Japanese garden with hardly any flowers. I drew Japanese people in business suits and teenagers in crazy clothes and several ladies in beautiful traditional kimonos. And right in the middle of them, looking very happy and interested, I drew Miss Lovejoy in her beige suit and flat shoes.

Mum and Dad let me stay up for half an hour past my bedtime to get it finished.

'Well done, darling! I'm sure Miss Lovejoy will be thrilled,' said Mum.

I was thrilled too. It was so lovely being able to draw. I don't want to sound like I'm boasting, but I can draw better than either Phil or Maddie. I've never been better than them at anything before.

I did wonder about drawing a picture for Selma too, but I decided she probably wouldn't want one. I didn't know what to give her for Christmas. This time last year I would never have dreamed

of giving Selma Johnson anything at all, but now
we were friends. Not *best* friends, but friends all
the same.

In the end I begged some
beads off Phil – blue and
green and purple, and five
alphabet beads – and made
Selma a bracelet.

On the last day of term I took Miss Lovejoy's
picture and Selma's bracelet in to school. Miss
Lovejoy had lots and lots of presents. Her desk
was completely covered. She looked very happy –
but she looked happiest of all when she took my
picture out of its envelope.

'Oh, Tina!' she said. 'Oh my goodness, the work
you've put into this! You must know more about
Japan than I do! It's beautiful.'

'Do you really, really like it? Might you hang it
on the wall beside my butterfly?'

'I'm not going to hang it in the classroom.'
Miss Lovejoy smiled at me. 'I shall hang it on my
bedroom wall at home, and then every day when I
wake up I shall see it and get excited about going

to Japan. Now I have a little something for you.'

She handed me an envelope. 'Don't get excited. It's not a present. It's not a donation for your butterfly garden – it's more the *promise* of one. Do you remember I suggested sponsoring you in a spelling test?'

'Oh, Miss Lovejoy! I hoped you were joking!'

'Inside the envelope you will find fifty words I know you can't spell. Learn them over Christmas. Then, the first day of term, I'll give you a test. I'll sponsor you fifty p a word. If you got them all right, then you'd get . . . how much for your butterfly garden?'

I fidgeted, trying to work it out.

'Oh dear, maths isn't your strong point either, Tina. Perhaps I'll set you an arithmetic test too!'

'Oh please, no! It's . . . it's . . .'

'Twenty-five pounds!' said Alistair.

'Alistair! I wanted Tina to work it out!' said Miss Lovejoy.

'Yes, I know, I couldn't help it. When I know the answer for something, I have to say it or burst!' he said.

'Twenty-five pounds!' I echoed, marvelling.

'But you have to get every single word right. Fifty p a word. It will mean a lot of hard work.'

'I'm used to hard work now,' I said. 'Right, Miss Lovejoy. You're on!'

Selma liked her Christmas present too. Very, very much. She put her bracelet on straight away and then kept lifting up her arm, showing it off to everyone. We weren't supposed to wear jewellery to school, but nobody minded on the last day of term.

'See my bracelet,' she kept saying to everyone.

'Of course I can see your bracelet. You're dangling it right under my nose!' Alistair told her.

'My friend Tina gave me it.'

'It's just a baby one she made from beads. It's not a proper bracelet from a shop,' said Kayleigh.

'It's better than a shop bracelet. Tina made it specially,' said Selma. 'You're just jealous.'

She turned to me. 'I need to tell you something when we're private.'

She waited until we were digging the very last piece of garden at playtime. Well, there was still quite a hard patch with a lot of bricks in the earth, but Miss Lovejoy said she might be able to come into school during the holidays and break it up a bit now that her back was better.

'Tina, I haven't got *you* a Christmas present,' said Selma.

'Never mind.'

'I feel bad about it. And the thing is, *you're* kind of my Christmas present,' she said.

'What do you mean?'

'I was having this conversation about Christmas with my mum, and she was asking me and my brother Sam what we want. Baby Joel's too little to ask because he can't talk yet. Sam was saying he wants all this stupid stuff, and *I* said all I really wanted was to have you come to tea one day.' Selma went red as she said it and wouldn't look at me.

'That's . . . lovely,' I said uncertainly. I liked Selma and I'd enjoyed having her to tea with me. I wasn't anywhere near as keen on the idea of going to tea with *her*. I didn't like the look of Selma's little brothers. Her mum seemed very fierce. And Selma herself said her stepdad could be really mean and scary. The more I thought about it, the more sure I was that I didn't want to go to tea with Selma at all – but I didn't want to hurt her feelings.

'You'll come then!' she said, suddenly looking radiant. 'How about this Saturday. Please say yes!'

'Well, I'll have to ask my mum . . .' I hesitated. 'She might not let me because – because I might have to help with all the Christmas shopping and that.'

'I'll ask her for you!' said Selma.

When all the mums came to collect us at the end of school, Selma charged across the playground, veered right round her own mum and threw herself at mine.

'Can Tina come to tea with me this Saturday?' she gabbled.

Mum looked taken aback. So did Phil and Maddie. Selma's mum looked surprised too.

'Well, that's very kind of you to ask her, dear, but . . .' Mum began, obviously searching for an excuse.

'I know you'll be busy doing Christmas stuff, but you've got Phil and Maddie to help. Oh, please let Tina come. She really wants to, don't you, Tina?' Selma nudged me, so I had to nod.

'But perhaps your mum will be busy too?' said mine, looking at Mrs Johnson.

'Yes, but I did promise our Selma,' she said. She had to speak loudly because Sam had snatched baby Joel's bottle and he was protesting bitterly. 'Shut up, you two pests! So, Saturday afternoon, at ours. We live at 93 Turner block, on the Painters Estate. Do you know where that is?'

Mum nodded. The Painters Estate was only two roads away from us but we'd never ever been there. The Painters Estate was famous for being ultra-scary.

'Perhaps we'd better see how Tina is on Saturday morning. I think she might be going down with another cold . . .' Mum started saying, but Mrs Johnson had already pushed off with Joel in the buggy, Sam yelling and Selma waving happily to me.

'Oh dear,' said Mum.

'You can't let our Tina go to tea with Selma!' said Phil.

'You'd be much too scared, wouldn't you, Tina?' said Maddie.

They both put their arms round me. I suddenly wriggled free. I *was* scared, but I didn't want to admit it. And Selma was my friend. She wanted me to go to tea with her so much, even more than a proper Christmas present.

'I want to go,' I said determinedly.

'I don't think that's a very good idea, Tina,' said Mum. 'It might be different if Phil and Maddie were invited too, but I don't like the thought of you going there on your own.'

'But you let Phil go to tea with Neera on her own. And Maddie went to the football match with Harry and his dad on her own,' I said.

'I know, but . . .' Mum didn't quite like to say

that she thought Selma and her family and her flat were scary. 'Let's see what Dad thinks,' she said.

She thought Dad would give a firm no and that would be that. But Dad was surprising.

'I think Tina should definitely go to tea with Selma,' he said.

'But I'm not sure she'll be all right. Selma's the girl who bullied her mercilessly at the start of term,' said Mum.

'Yes, but she doesn't any more, does she? She seemed a nice little kiddie when she came to tea with us. My dad took a real shine to her. I bet our Tina will have a whale of a time if we let her go. You're getting really fond of Selma, aren't you, lovey?' Dad put his arm round me and I nodded – though there was still a little part of me that wanted him to stop me going.

But it was all decided. I was going to tea with Selma on Saturday.

Phil and Maddie and I always wore our play clothes on Saturday. We had sweatshirts in different colours (Phil had blue, Maddie had red and I had green) and dungarees with little pockets. I liked my dungarees, but I always felt a bit sad when I put them on now, because I used to carry Baby around in the pocket.

I thought about Baby all morning. I didn't want to eat much lunch. And at half past two, when Mum said we'd better be going, I suddenly blurted out, 'I don't think I want to go to tea with Selma after all!'

'Oh, Tina, *now* you tell me!' said Mum. 'Well, it's too late to change your mind. I expect you'll have a lovely time when you get there.'

'I don't think I will!' I said in a tiny voice.

'Poor Tina,' said Phil, putting her arm round me. 'Don't make her go, Mum.'

'Poor Tina,' said Maddie, putting *her* arm round me. 'Even *I* would be a bit worried about going to tea with Selma.'

'Oh, you girls, stop ganging up on me,' said Mum. 'Now come on. We'll walk Tina to the Painters Estate and see how she feels about it when we get there. If you're still absolutely certain you don't want to go, then we'll knock on Selma's door and politely explain that you don't feel very well. You do look a bit peaky, sweetheart.'

I felt even less well when we got to the Painters Estate. Phil and Maddie and I held hands tightly. There were gangs of boys on skateboards whizzing past so near that we all jumped. There were gangs of big girls who all mocked us and called rude names. Mum told them off and they all shrieked with laughter and called her even ruder names.

'Right, that's it!' she said. 'Come on, girls, we're going home.'

But just then we heard someone calling up above us.

'*Tina! Tina! Hey, Tina!!!*' It was Selma, hanging

over a high-up walkway, waving and yelling excitedly. 'Wait there – I'll come and get you!'

So we had to wait. Selma came charging out of the lift and threw her arms round me. 'You came! I was so worried you wouldn't really come! And we're going to have a really special tea. Come on up!' she said.

'Oh dear, Selma,' said Mum. 'I'm so sorry, but I think Tina's feeling a bit poorly. I would have phoned your mother, but I don't have her phone number. I'm not sure Tina's well enough to come to tea.'

Selma's face crumpled.

I couldn't bear it. 'Yes I am, Mum,' I said. 'You come and get me later, OK? Come on, Selma.'

And we ran off together, hand in hand.

Chapter Nineteen

Selma's flat was amazing. I'd thought it would be sad and threadbare because Selma didn't have nice clothes and never had any money to spare. I was so wrong!

She had a television that was very nearly as big as the living-room wall. It was just like going to the cinema! There was also a television in the kitchen, and another one in Selma and Sam's bedroom. We only had one television in our house and it was quite small.

She had two great big leather sofas, practically brand-new, and as soft as butter so you could sink down into them. There was a matching big black leather chair with its own soft black leather footstool. We only had one sofa, and it was a terrible squash if Mum and Dad and Phil and Maddie and I all tried to sit on it together. Our chairs didn't match and we didn't even have a footstool.

Everything matched in Selma's flat. The towels in the bathroom were the same design, just different sizes, and they matched the fluffy bath mat. All our towels at home were different colours and our bath mat wasn't fluffy any more. I had a peep in Selma's mum's room, and she had amazing matching leopard-print bedcovers. Baby Joel's cot was there too. He had a jungle print on his little baby duvet, and a big toy leopard crouched on his pillow.

I thought Selma's bedroom would be magic too, but she had to share with her brother Sam, and it was a bit messy and crowded with all his toys. They didn't have matching duvets. Sam had Postman Pat. Maddie used to have that exact duvet cover. Selma had a pink fairy one. She blushed when she saw me staring.

'I've had that stupid duvet cover since I was little. It's sooooo babyish,' she said quickly.

'I think it's lovely. I wish *I* had a fairy duvet,' I said.

Selma had a fairy musical box too, but it wouldn't play when I tried turning the handle.

'Sam broke it,' she told me.

She had a fairy doll too, but its hair had been chopped off and its face scribbled on.

'Did Sam do that too?' I asked.

'I can't stick Sam. Or Joel. Or their stupid dad,' said Selma.

We couldn't play in Selma's bedroom because Sam came in too, and he mucked about and spoiled all our games.

'You shove off, squirt,' said Selma.

'Won't! It's my bedroom too, wobble-bum!' he said.

Selma tried to push him out. He kicked and spat at her. She pushed a bit harder and he fell over. He didn't really hurt himself but he started yelling.

'I'll tell my dad on you,' he said, sticking out his chin.

'See if I care, telltale,' said Selma.

He wouldn't leave us in peace, so we left the bedroom and locked ourselves in the bathroom. It was much more peaceful. Selma's mum kept her make-up in the bathroom cabinet, so Selma and I had a grand time putting on eyeliner and shadow and lipstick. We looked almost like grown-up ladies.

'But we'd better wash it all off or my mum will do her nut,' said Selma.

We washed it off as best we could. Some of the eye stuff ended up on the towel, but Selma shoved it into the dirty clothes basket. Then we played making soap bubbles in the basin with the bar of Lux. We pretended we were ladies in a telly advert. Selma actually lay in the empty bath, pretending she was soaping herself all over. We didn't half get the giggles.

Sam started whining outside, saying he was desperate for a wee.

Eventually Mrs Johnson came knocking at the

door. 'Come on, you two! Out you come. Let the kid in or he'll wet all over my shag carpet.'

We got the giggles even more, spluttering as we came out.

'You two – *cackle cackle cackle*!' said Mrs Johnson, but she wasn't really cross.

We all went into the living room and watched a DVD together. Mum only lets Phil and Maddie and me watch children's films, but this was a totally grown-up drama, and it was really scary. Mrs Johnson didn't seem to mind us watching. Sam whooped with excitement whenever any men did something really bad. Baby Joel crawled around happily, not seeming to mind all the shouting and thumping on the screen.

I tried not to watch properly, screwing up my eyes whenever it got really violent.

'You OK, Tina?' Selma asked. 'Great film, isn't it?'

'Yes, great,' I said weakly.

It was a relief when Selma's stepdad came in and we stopped watching the film. I thought he might be very mean and scary – I knew Selma didn't like him at all – but he seemed really jolly and friendly at first.

'So you're little Teeny Tiny Tears!' he said to me. 'My goodness, you're small enough to fit into my pocket. Fancy a little tiddler like you being friends with our great girl Selma!'

'Hello, Mr Johnson,' I said shyly.

'I'm not Mr Johnson, sweetheart. I'm Mr Barlow, but you can call me Jason. Lovely manners, you've got. You could teach our Selma a lesson.'

Selma glared at him.

'See what I mean!' said Jason. 'Face like thunder whenever I come in! Still, you're pleased to see me, aren't you, boys?'

He picked up little Joel and tickled him until he squealed, and then mock-wrestled with Sam.

'Watch the furniture, you lot!' said Mrs Johnson. 'Well, I suppose I'd better get tea organized.'

She didn't do any cooking. She just phoned up the pizza parlour and ordered five barbecue chicken melt pizzas, with six twisted dough balls, two big tubs of cookie-dough ice cream and three big bottles of Coke. I listened with my mouth open. Mum only lets Phil and Maddie and me have cheese and tomato pizzas, and we have to share one between the three of us. I'd never had dough balls or cookie-dough ice cream, and I was only allowed Coke as a special party treat. Oh, I was soooo glad I'd decided to go to tea with Selma.

I liked her so much now. Maybe I hoped she'd become my best friend after all. Her mum was very nice to me too. Sam was a bit of a pain, but Joel was all right, though you got dribbled on if he came too near you. I thought Selma's stepdad was sort of OK, though I didn't like the way he talked to her.

He was all right when he talked to *me*. In fact,

he made a special effort to chat to me, asking me all about my sisters.

'It must be fun to be a triplet,' he said. 'Especially if your sisters are both as sweet as you. Not too sure how we'd cope if Selma was one of three though!'

'Not sure how *I'd* cope if *you* were triplets,' said Selma, sticking out her chin.

'Here! Watch that lip!' said Jason. 'Or else!'

Perhaps I didn't like him after all. But I tried hard to be polite, hoping he wouldn't get really mad with Selma. I nattered on about the butterfly garden, telling him how wonderful Selma had been, digging the whole garden almost by herself.

'Our Selma? Well, that's a surprise! She certainly doesn't make herself useful at home,' said Jason.

'You wouldn't know,' said Selma. 'You're hardly

ever at home, thank goodness. You're always down the pub or the betting shop.'

My tummy went tight.

Jason glared at her. 'I'm telling you, madam – you talk to me like that one more time and it's bed for you, whether you've got your sweet little friend to tea or not,' he said.

Selma swallowed. I willed her not to say another word.

Luckily Sam started acting up, throwing the cushions around and jumping on them.

'Hey! Leave off, you little monster!' said Mrs Johnson.

'And I'm Big Daddy Monster and I'm going to get you if you don't behave!' said Jason, and he started crawling on the floor, pulling faces and making growling noises.

Sam shrieked with laughter. Jason started wrestling with him and they rolled over and over. I stared at them, wondering why Jason let the boys get away with murder and yet was so picky with Selma. I looked at her and she rolled her eyes at me.

Then we heard the doorbell. The pizzas were here – and the dough balls and the cookie-dough ice cream and the Cokes. We didn't have to sit at the table with plates and knives and forks. We just sat where we were and ate  out of the containers. It was much more fun.

Mrs Johnson and Jason and Selma and I all had a pizza each, and a dough ball and a glass of Coke. (The ice cream was put in the freezer for afterwards.) Sam had three-quarters of a pizza, and a dough ball and a mug of Coke. Baby Joel had quarter of a pizza, and a dough ball and a bottle of Coke.

I *loved* my pizza – apart from the onions, which were a bit slimy. I decided I was going to eat the whole thing (apart from the onions). I'd be able to boast to Phil and Maddie. But the more I ate, the bigger the pizza seemed to grow. The onions grew too. I was scared to bite into each slice in case I got a mouthful of onion.

Selma saw me hesitating. 'What's up? Don't

you like it?' she asked, while the others were all busy thumping baby Joel on the back because his pizza had gone down the wrong way.

'I don't like onions,' I hissed.

'Never mind. Look, I'll eat your onions,' Selma offered. She started picking out all my onions while I smiled at her gratefully.

'What are you doing, Selma?' Jason asked sharply. 'Leave Tina's pizza alone! Haven't you got enough of your own?'

'It's all right, Jason, she's just taking my onions. I don't like them very much,' I said quickly.

'See!' said Selma. 'You've always got to stick your big nose in.' Then she called Jason a rude word. She only muttered that bit under her breath, but I heard what she said. And he did too.

'Right! That's it! Get to bed!' said Jason.

'Oh, Jason, let the kid eat her pizza!' said Mrs Johnson.

'I warned her. Get!' Jason shouted, and he pulled Selma to her feet and pushed her towards the door.

She started crying then and he mocked her,

pretending to cry himself. Sam thought this was very funny and roared with laughter. I felt sick.

Then Selma was gone and I was left alone in the living room with this strange family.

'Eat up, little Tina,' said Jason, his voice normal now. 'You didn't want Selma mucking about with your food, did you?'

I didn't dare contradict him, though I felt terribly disloyal to Selma. Her own pizza and dough ball grew cold. I struggled to eat more of mine, but it was difficult with my stomach in knots. I took a mouthful of onions and heaved.

'Please may I go to the bathroom?' I gabbled, and shot out of the room.

I *was* a bit sick. I'd never been sick on my own before. Mum or Dad had always held my forehead and mopped me up afterwards. I had to wash my face and take a drink of water all by myself.

When I'd stopped shaking and felt a little better, I let myself out of the bathroom very quietly and tiptoed along the carpet to Selma's bedroom. Her door was open and I could hear muffled sobbing.

I crept right up to her door and went into her room. Selma was curled up in a ball on her bed, tears dripping down her face. She was holding something in her hand, whispering.

I went nearer, wondering what it was.

I could just see a little head poking out of Selma's hand. A little china head.

'*Baby!*' I said.

Selma jumped. She shoved her hand under her pillow. 'What?' she mumbled.

'That's Baby! My Baby! You had her all the time!' I said. 'You didn't flush her down the loo, you *stole* her!'

'No I didn't! What Baby? I haven't got any flipping Baby – see?' Selma showed me two empty hands.

But she knew and I knew that Baby was under her pillow.

'Give me back Baby! I thought you were my friend! We've been friends for months and you kept her all this time!' I said.

'You're mad! I haven't got no Baby! Look, get out of my room, Little Bug,' Selma shouted.

'Hey, hey!' It was Jason. 'Are you two having an argy-bargy now? What's she said to you, Tina? I'll soon give her what for!'

Selma looked at me. Her nose was running as well as her eyes. I was furious with her and I was desperate to get Baby back, but I couldn't tell on her.

'She hasn't done anything,' I said, and then I burst into tears too.

Chapter Twenty

I didn't tell Mum when she came to collect me. I didn't want to talk about any of it. I just bent my head and didn't answer when she asked if I'd had a good time.

She gave me a hug. 'I don't think you did,' she said. 'Never mind. You don't ever have to go again, not if you don't want to.'

Phil and Maddie were much more inquisitive, though they waited until we were all in bed.

They were seriously impressed when I said I'd had a barbecue chicken melt pizza and a dough ball and a glass of Coke. (I couldn't eat the cookie-dough ice cream because I was so upset.)

They shivered when I told them about Jason and how scary he could be.

'I think I'm starting to feel sorry for Selma,' said Phil.

'It must be awful to have a stepdad who doesn't like you,' agreed Maddie.

'Yes, but then I found out something. Selma *stole* Baby!' I told them.

'You already know that, silly,' said Phil.

'She flushed her down the toilet,' said Maddie.

'No, she didn't! She just *pretended* to. She must have shoved her up her sleeve or in her pocket or something when she was inside the toilet cubicle. Because she's still got her. I saw! She was holding her, and it was definitely Baby, but she wouldn't give her back. She hid her again and pretended I was mistaken, but I wasn't. She's kept Baby all this time, even though she was my friend and knows how much I miss her,' I wailed.

'Oh, Tina, you poor thing,' said Phil.

'Don't worry. When school goes back we'll

confront her and *make* her give Baby back,' said Maddie.

'I don't think I want her to be my friend any more,' I said.

'Well, you don't need her as a friend – you've got us,' said Phil.

'But you've got Neera for your friend now,' I pointed out.

'Yes, Neera's my best friend, and Maddie's got Harry as her best friend, but you two are my *bestest* best friends,' said Phil. 'Isn't that right, Maddie?'

'Of course it is,' said Maddie. 'We're Phil and Tina and me.'

'We're Maddie and Tina and me,' said Phil.

'We're Phil and Maddie and me,' I said, and I felt so very glad that I had my two sisters.

It was lovely to be on holiday. Phil and Maddie and I helped Mum make a Christmas cake and we all had a go at stirring. We made our own Christmas cards and went shopping to buy presents.

We clubbed together to buy a purse for Mum and a pen for Dad and a lipstick for Gran and woolly socks for Grandad. We went into the toy shop one by one to buy presents for each other. I bought a little plastic pony for Phil and a bag of marbles for Maddie. I tried not to think of the plants I could have bought instead of presents!

I also spent half an hour every single day trying to learn my spellings. Miss Lovejoy had given me the list of fifty words.

I copied each one out five times. It was very, very tedious. Then Phil and Maddie tested me. I didn't get them all right. In fact, most of the time I got them wrong, and then I got upset, because I so wanted to get lots of money for my butterfly garden. Mum and Dad were sponsoring me too. And Gran and Grandad and Mrs Richards next door. I tried and tried to learn the words, staring at them until the letters wiggled around and didn't make sense at all.

Mum tried helping me. And Dad. If anything, it made me worse: I was so anxious to please them that my mind went fuzzy and I couldn't even spell baby words like 'the' or 'and'.

On Christmas Day Gran and Grandad came over and stayed till Boxing Day. Christmas was lovely, of course. Mum and Dad gave Phil and Maddie and me three scooters – one each!!! Gran gave us all princess dressing-up clothes with silver slippers with little heels. Grandad gave us another massive Lego set, and we started building it on Christmas afternoon and Boxing Day morning.

Guess what Phil and Maddie gave me! Phil had bought me a little plastic baby doll and Maddie had bought two sets of clothes for her – a dress and coat and hat set, and a dressing gown and nightie set.

'She's a new Baby for you,' they said.

'Thank you! Oh, I love her!' I said.

I didn't love her as much as my first real Baby, and although she was small, she wasn't as little as Baby so she couldn't hide in my hand – but she was very sweet, and it was very, very kind of my sisters to buy her for me.

I didn't try to learn my spellings on Christmas Day, of course, but I did get the dreaded list out on Boxing Day.

'How are you doing, pet?' asked Grandad. 'How much money am I going to have to fork out?'

'I don't think you'll have to fork out a single penny, Grandad,' I said miserably. 'I just can't learn the wretched things.'

'Let me see, sweetheart . . .' Grandad got out his reading glasses and peered. 'Oh dear. Yes, I remember learning some of these chappies when *I* was at school. You know what I did? I made up funny little songs for the hardest words. Let's see. E-g-y-p-t-i-a-n. *Egyptian*. Sing it with me.'

295

I sang it. Phil and Maddie sang it too. I had it by heart in about thirty seconds.

'There! Now, write it down quickly, Tina,' said Grandad.

I did, singing the song inside my head – and for the first time the 'g's and 'y's and 'p's came out the right way round.

'I *like* spelling this way, Grandad!' I said happily.

'Tina's got our names on her spelling list, Grandad. Can you make up a song for *Philippa*?'

'Certainly. Let's think. P-h-i-l-i-p-p-a. How about that?' He made it a lovely pretty plinky song, just right for *Philippa*. Then he made up Maddie's song. 'M-a-d-e-l-e-i-n-e. *Madeleine*.' He made it funny and shouty, a bit like a football song.

By the time Grandad went home on Boxing Day evening he'd made up songs for half my list, and I could remember most of them. He came back later on in the Christmas holidays to remind me of the tunes I'd forgotten, and made up lots more.

I went around singing my spelling songs over and over again. I sang at breakfast, I sang when we were riding our scooters up and down the pavement, I sang while we were building with the Lego, I sang while we were playing games on our iPad, I sang while we had lunch, I sang when we went to the shops, I sang when I played with New Baby and our Monster High dolls, I sang when we were feeding Nibbles and Speedy and Cheesepuff, I sang when we had tea, I sang while we were watching television, I sang when we went to bed.

'You might be learning how to spell, but all that singing doesn't half get annoying at times,' said Phil.

'If I didn't know how much your butterfly garden means to you, I'd put this pillow over your head to smother you. I'll just give you a whack with it instead,' said Maddie, doing just that.

So that started a pillow fight, and we all shrieked with laughter, whacking and whacking and whacking, until suddenly Maddie's pillow split open and showered us with feathers. They flew everywhere – over the beds, the carpet, the dolls on the windowsill, our hamsters in their cage – looking like little butterflies fluttering around. We watched, enchanted and appalled, until Mum came in and told us off big-time.

I even dreamed my spelling words. They drifted around inside my head all night, just like the feathers. During the day I wrote them down in different colours, using the set of pens Miss Lovejoy had given me.

I also watched *Ruby Red* on the television.

'What do you want to watch such a baby programme for?' asked Maddie, snatching the remote to change the channel.

'Oh, let her. She can't help being a bit young for her age,' said Phil.

'I'm *not* young for my age. I just like *Ruby Red*,' I said.

Ruby talked about Christmas and dressed up

as Santa Claus, and told us to send in pictures of our favourite present. In another episode she talked about zoos and pretended to be different animals, and then asked us for pictures of elephants and giraffes and monkeys. The next day she talked about food, and made rock buns, and told us to send her a picture of our favourite cake. There were so many *Ruby Red* programmes and I loved them all. I longed to draw her a picture, but there wasn't time. I was too busy spelling.

Then it was time to go back to school again. I suddenly felt scared, as if it was my first day in the Juniors all over again. I was really worried about seeing Selma. I didn't know how to react. I still felt so angry that she had secretly kept Baby all that time – but I also felt sorry for her, living with such a mean stepdad. I kept thinking of her face, all sad and tear-stained, and it made my stomach go upside down.

I was also scared of forgetting my spellings when Miss Lovejoy tested me. I knew them all, but now each night I dreamed that when it came to the test they all flew out of my ears and I was left not being able to spell a single one.

'I don't feel well, Mum,' I said at breakfast. It was true. I felt hot and yet shivery, and too sick to eat anything.

Mum felt my forehead and looked anxious. 'Oh dear, don't say you're going down with something your first day back at school!' she said.

'I think Tina's just a bit worried about school, that's all,' said Dad. 'I always used to get the collywobbles on *my* first day back.'

Collywobbles was such a funny word I couldn't help laughing, and then I *did* feel a bit better.

'Don't worry, Tina. You'll do brilliantly when Miss Lovejoy tests you,' said Phil. 'You're a much better speller than Maddie or me now.'

'And don't worry about Selma,' Maddie whispered. 'We'll get your old Baby back, and we'll bash her up for stealing her.'

'I'm not sure I'll remember my spellings. And I don't want Selma bashed up. She's still my friend – at least I think she is.'

But when we got to the playground Selma

didn't come over to say hello. The moment she saw us she marched off and stood right at the other end.

'There! She isn't your friend any more,' said Maddie.

Selma wouldn't even talk to me in class. We still sat on the same table, but she didn't once lean over Alistair and talk to me the way she used to.

'It's surprisingly peaceful now,' said Alistair.

It was too quiet. I didn't like it at all, especially when I saw Selma talking to Kayleigh. Was she going to be Kayleigh's friend again?

I decided to have it out with her at playtime,

but Miss Lovejoy collared me the second the bell went.

'Not so fast, Tina. You and I have to attend to a little spelling test. Remember?'

'Oh. A spelling test,' I said, as if I hadn't thought about it all holiday.

'Oh dear, haven't you been practising?' Miss Lovejoy looked disappointed.

'A little bit,' I said.

'Well, just do your best,' she told me. 'Now, does anyone else want to keep Tina company doing a very hard spelling test, or would you sooner go out and play?'

Naturally they all made for the classroom door. Phil and Maddie dithered as they went out.

'Would you like us to stay, Tina?' asked Phil.

'We will if you really want us to,' said Maddie.

Selma didn't offer to stay. She'd already gone. Yet it was going to be just as much her butterfly garden as mine.

I felt hurt and angry. All right, I'd spell all by myself. I shook my head at dear kind Phil and Maddie.

'You go and play,' I said. 'I'll be fine.'

'That's the spirit, Tina.' Miss Lovejoy poured herself a cup of tea from a vacuum flask and opened a packet of chocolate biscuits. 'Excuse me having my playtime snack. Would you like a biscuit to nibble on too?'

That made me feel a bit better. My insides were starting to feel horribly wobbly and empty. What if I couldn't remember any of the spellings, like in my dreams? I tried to run through them in my head, but they were all jumbled up.

Miss Lovejoy got out her long list. 'Let's begin. Spell *little*.'

That wasn't fair. *Little* wasn't first on the list. It should be *Philippa* and then *Madeleine*. I couldn't do it if she didn't ask the words in the right order.

Then I thought of Grandad. 'Yes, you can do it, pet,' he said inside my head. 'Just think of the song, remember.'

Little had a teeny tiny song in a whispery voice,

because it was a little word. I wrote it down quickly while I remembered it.

Remember was the next word. I always used to put in too many 'm's and 'b's. But Grandad had sung it in a jerky, funny way – r-e-m-e-m-b-e-r – so that *remember* was easy-peasy to remember! I wrote it down.

I wrote down all fifty of the words. We were still working our way through them when the bell rang. Miss Lovejoy made the class sit down quietly and do silent reading while we carried on.

Alistair tried to whisper the correct spellings to me. He was only being helpful but it started to confuse me.

'Alistair, I have a roll of sellotape in my desk drawer. Don't make me have to seal your lips up,' said Miss Lovejoy.

She was only joking, but Alistair shut up quick. I carried on writing word after word until the very last one – finished!

'There, Tina. I'm glad you attempted each and every one. Hand me your workbook and I'll check them through at lunch time. Now, everyone, let's turn to arithmetical matters. Multiplication and division!'

They were two of my spelling words. I thought I knew how to spell them properly now, but I still struggled terribly *doing* multiplication and division, and I definitely needed Alistair's help.

'There were some truly awesomely difficult spellings on that list,' he said. 'I think I might have struggled with one or two.'

'One or two!' said Mick. 'I could hardly do any.'

 'How many do you think you got right, Tina?' Peter asked.

'Bet you hardly got any right – you're a hopeless speller,' said Kayleigh nastily.

305

Selma said nothing at all. She wouldn't even look at me. It was as if I didn't exist any more. I noticed she wasn't wearing the special bracelet I'd made for her.

The moment the bell went for lunch she rushed out of the classroom. But we rushed too – Phil and Maddie and me. She was much quicker than me, but Phil nearly caught her up – and Maddie went charging past and cornered her.

'Now listen here, Selma. You've got our Tina's Baby and you've jolly well got to give her back!' said Maddie.

'Don't know what you're talking about,' she said.

'Yes you do!' Phil puffed. 'Tina saw you holding her little china doll.'

'That was *my* one. I flushed her little dolly down the toilet,' said Selma.

'It was *my* Baby, Selma – I saw where I'd crayoned on her. I know she was mine,' I said.

'Yeah, but you also know I threw her away. So make up your mind, stupid Little Bug,' said Selma, and she suddenly dodged round Maddie and ran for it down the corridor.

'It *was* Baby, I know it was,' I said sadly.

'We could go after her and bash her,' said Maddie.

'No we can't. You know we can't hit people – and besides, Selma might hit back even harder,' said Phil. 'Oh dear, poor Tina. Still, at least you've got New Baby now.'

'And New Baby has real clothes. She's much more fun to play with,' said Maddie.

'Yes,' I agreed. Privately I didn't think New Baby was a patch on my old Baby, but I couldn't say that as they'd bought her for me as a special Christmas present. And I didn't really want to think about *any* Babies, old or new. I was too worried about the results of my spelling test.

'I'm scared I haven't got any of the words right,' I said in a tiny voice.

'Of course you have. I bet you get nearly all of them right,' said Phil. 'You did ever so well in our tests.'

'Yes, but Miss Lovejoy muddled up the list. I didn't know where I was. And I couldn't sing the spellings out loud – it wasn't the same doing them inside my head. What if I've got them all wrong?'

'You must have got *some* of them right,' said Maddie. 'You're such a worry-pot, Tina.'

'I just so want to get compost and plants for the butterfly garden,' I said.

'You've already got heaps of money from the cake sale and the Christmas fete. And you know Grandad will give you money even if you don't get *any* spellings right,' said Maddie.

I was so worried about it that I could hardly eat any of my lunch, even though Mum had put in little red cheeses and a tiny bunch of grapes and a banana sandwich and baby pots of strawberry yoghurt as special going-back-to-school treats.

Miss Lovejoy had said she'd mark my spellings at lunch time, but when we went back into the classroom for afternoon school she didn't even mention them! She just got stuck into lessons immediately.

I could barely concentrate. I wondered about sticking my hand up and asking her outright, but

I couldn't summon the courage. I just sat there miserably, with all the spelling songs jangling around in my head.

But ten minutes before the bell was due to go for the end of school Miss Lovejoy suddenly clapped her hands. 'Right, put your books away, children, and sit up straight. I have an announcement to make.'

We all did as we were told, wondering what was going on.

'Now, I don't expect you've failed to notice that Tina Maynard here is rather keen to establish a butterfly garden at school,' said Miss Lovejoy.

There were a few giggles and groans.

'Tina and Selma have worked very hard digging up the patch of earth at the end of the playground,' she went on.

I glanced at Selma. Her head was bent. Perhaps she wasn't even listening.

'They've raised a considerable sum of money already. I decided to help Tina by sponsoring her in a spelling test. Tina has always found spelling rather a challenge ...'

I bent my head now too. Perhaps I'd done really badly and Miss Lovejoy was about to brandish my workbook with numerous red crosses and the whole class would laugh at me. I longed to be sitting in between Phil and Maddie so they could hold my hands.

'Tina sat the spelling test this morning and now I have marked it. I want you all to guess how many spellings she has got right,' said Miss Lovejoy.

'None!' said Kayleigh.

'I'm sure she's got at least half right, maybe more,' said Phil.

'She should have got lots and lots right – she worked so hard at it all holiday,' said Maddie.

'Perhaps she got seventy-five per cent correct?' suggested Alistair.

'I'm afraid you're all one hundred per cent wrong,' said Miss Lovejoy, 'because Tina has got one hundred per cent of her spellings right!'

I looked up, a little dazed. I wasn't totally sure what she meant. She didn't mean . . . she couldn't mean . . .

'Yes, Tina! You got every single spelling right, all fifty words!' she said.

Everyone gasped and clapped. Phil and Maddie cheered.

'I feel like cheering too,' said Miss Lovejoy. 'You've done extremely well. I've shown your work-book to all the other teachers. They've felt inspired to sponsor you too. My handbag is quite weighed down with all their donations. And I am going to keep my word. Fifty correct spellings equals a whole twenty-five pounds!'

Chapter Twenty-One

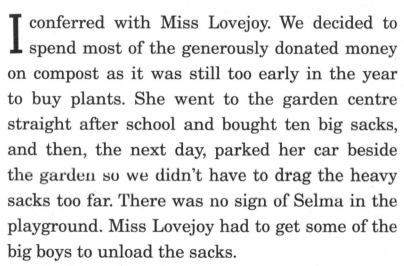

I conferred with Miss Lovejoy. We decided to spend most of the generously donated money on compost as it was still too early in the year to buy plants. She went to the garden centre straight after school and bought ten big sacks, and then, the next day, parked her car beside the garden so we didn't have to drag the heavy sacks too far. There was no sign of Selma in the playground. Miss Lovejoy had to get some of the big boys to unload the sacks.

'We'll start digging in the compost at lunch time,' she said.

'Thank you soooo much, Miss Lovejoy,' I said.

When the bell rang for lunch, Selma rushed off with the others.

'Selma!' Miss Lovejoy called. 'Where are you going?'

'I don't think she wants to do the garden any more,' I said, 'but it's all right. I'll do all the digging, I don't mind.'

'Did you hear that, Selma?' said Miss Lovejoy. 'Do you think Tina will manage the digging by herself?'

Selma shrugged. 'You'll help her, miss.'

'Miss *Lovejoy*. I'll only be able to dig for a little while. My back's still playing up and I have to be very cautious. *You're* the expert digger, Selma. So strong. Ten times stronger than little Tina here. Don't you want to help her?'

'She don't want me to,' said Selma.

'Don't be silly, of course she does. And *I* want you to dig too. So come along.'

The three of us went out to the garden and started digging the compost in, bag by bag. It was long, slow, heavy, messy work. I had

to rest every few minutes so I didn't get too tired. Selma did most of the digging, getting so hot she had to take off her coat and roll up her sleeves.

Miss Lovejoy said she must have a rest too. 'Sit down with Tina and you can both eat your packed lunches. It will give you a bit more energy – although you've been better than a JCB attacking that earth, Selma! Well done. Now I'm going off to the staff room to have *my* lunch,' she said.

I didn't want her to go. It was so awkward being with Selma now that we weren't friends any more. She sat at one end of the garden eating her bag of crisps. I sat at the other nibbling on my egg-and-tomato sandwich. We didn't look at each other.

I had to see whether Selma was talking to me at all.

'Do you like egg-and-tomato sandwiches?' I asked.

She went on munching crisps and didn't reply for several seconds. 'Not much,' she said eventually.

'Oh,' I said. 'It's just that I can't eat all mine.'

Selma peered over at my open lunch box. She saw a purple wrapper. 'I do like chocolate though,' she said.

Mum had put the chocolate bar in my lunch box as a special treat. She rarely let us have chocolate.

'Would you like half of my bar?' I asked, after an inner struggle.

'Yes!' Selma came over and sat beside me.

I broke the bar in half and we ate our pieces of chocolate together. In silence, still not looking at each other. Then Selma mumbled something.

'What did you say?'

'I said thanks,' she repeated.

'Oh. That's fine. You're sure you don't want half a sandwich too?'

'Well, if you don't want it, then OK.'

Selma steadily ate her way through the rest of my lunch. Then she mumbled thanks again.

'I should be thanking you for doing all that digging. You've got ever so dirty,' I said, looking at the earth splattered all over Selma's socks and shoes.

She shrugged again. 'They weren't clean on anyway,' she said.

We sat in silence.

'Well. Better get on with this mucky old compost,' said Selma. 'Still, at least I'm good at something.'

I thought of her life at home, where she was always the bad girl, no matter what she did. I thought of her lying on her bed, crying.

'Yes. Selma . . . about Baby . . .' I said.

Selma scowled. 'I don't know what you mean. I *haven't* got her,' she said in a rush.

'Maybe I made a mistake. But – but if you *did* happen to have her, then it's all right. I've got a new Baby now. Phil and Maddie gave her to me for Christmas. So we could have a Baby each, see?' I said.

Selma scowled even more. Then I saw why. Her eyes were brimming with tears. She was struggling not to cry. I reached out and took hold of her hand. I squeezed it tightly and she squeezed mine back.

We didn't say any more. We didn't need to. We were friends again.

Phil and Maddie were quite irritated with me when they realized this.

'Honestly, Tina, why do you want to stay friends with her when she's been so mean to you?' asked Phil when we were going to bed. 'She wasn't even talking to you earlier.'

'Yes, I know, but I think it was just because she was a bit sad and embarrassed,' I said.

'No wonder! She stole your Baby and let you think she was lost for ever!' said Maddie.

'Yes, I know, but maybe she needs Baby more than me. She hasn't got *any* nice dolls. Her little brother spoils them all.'

'*I'd* spoil them all if I had Selma as a big sister!' said Maddie. 'You're nuts wanting such a mean girl to stay friends with you.'

'It's because Tina's never made any friends of her own before,' said Phil. 'She's prepared to put up with anything even though it's silly.'

'It's not a bit silly!' I said, flaring up. 'I like Selma. And she still likes me, so you two can just shut up.'

'You're getting mean too,' said Maddie. 'Selma's meanness is rubbing off on you!'

I pushed her.

'Don't, Tina!' said Phil.

'There! She's trying to beat me up now, just like Selma!' said Maddie.

'No, *this* is beating you up!' I started mock-punching her.

'And this is a real fight!' said Maddie, play-punching back.

'And this is a wrestle!' said Phil, grabbing hold of both of us.

We ended up rolling on the floor in a great tangle, shrieking with laughter.

'Hey, hey, what's going on, girls?' Mum and Dad came running into the room.

'Phil, Maddie, get off your sister this minute!' Mum shouted. 'You know perfectly well that Tina mustn't romp about like that!'

'Tina started it, Mum! And we're not *really* fighting.' Phil struggled to her feet.

'Tina's been beating both of us up!' Maddie spluttered.

'Now stop being silly, all of you. Tina, are you all right?' Mum hauled me up and peered at me anxiously.

'Of course she's all right,' said Dad. 'How do you spell *right*, Champion Speller?'

'R-i-g-h-t!' I sang.

'Good girl! Even though you've cost us all a fortune,' said Dad. 'So when are you going to buy all these plants then?'

'Miss Lovejoy says it's a bit too early still.

We've got to wait till it gets warmer. Then she's going to take Selma and me to a garden centre.'

'My, she's certainly going the extra mile for you girls.'

'Tina and Selma are her favourites,' said Phil.

'She lets them get away with murder,' said Maddie.

'No she doesn't. She's still strict with us and bosses us about. But I think she does like us,' I said.

'No wonder,' said Dad.

'Is Tina *your* favourite, Dad?' Maddie asked.

'I think she's *Mum's* favourite,' said Phil.

'What nonsense!' said Mum and Dad together, laughing.

'You're all three our favourites,' said Dad, giving us all a big hug.

'Favourite girls in all the world – so long as you hop into bed this minute and fall fast asleep,' said Mum.

I had a new way of getting myself to sleep now. Inside my head I made lists of all the plants that butterflies liked. I knew that I needed a buddleia – maybe two or even three, because my butterfly book said that butterflies needed mass planting. There were different kinds of buddleia, and they came in many different colours too – purples and blues and pinks and white.

I needed spring flowers – primulas and aubretia and bugle. Summer flowers like sweet william and lavender and red valerian and asters.

I needed autumn flowers like Michaelmas daisies.

I also needed dandelions and nettles, but Selma said she'd dig some up from the grounds of her estate for nothing. And I could do with some rotten fruit too – but perhaps I could simply chuck a few old apples and oranges around the garden for the butterflies to snack on. I didn't have time to grow fruit trees.

I turned my butterfly plant list into a little song.

Butterflies, butterflies
Come eat my buddleia
Purple and blue and white
Pink that's very bright
Primula, aubretia, bugle too

Asters and lavender's blue
Sweet william and valerian red
Remember all the plants I've said
And Michaelmas daisies
Sing their praises.

In March Miss Lovejoy took Selma and me to buy the plants at the garden centre. She had all our money in a big purse. We went in the school minibus after lessons finished. She promised our mums she'd drive us home afterwards.

I sang my list of plants, and Miss Lovejoy steered us to all the right sections and we found nearly everything – though they said we'd have to come back later in the year for the Michaelmas daisies. We piled all our plants up in a great big trolley.

'Let me push it, Miss Lovejoy, or you'll do your back in again,' said Selma.

'You're such a helpful girl, Selma,' said Miss Lovejoy.

Selma beamed at her.

It was a bit scary spending our money in one go. Such a *lot* of money.

'If we'd had more time we could have grown a lot of the plants from seed, but it took such ages to get the earth ready,' I said.

'I think you two did a great job,' said Miss Lovejoy. 'All that digging did you both a lot of good.'

'We'd never have become friends otherwise,' I said.

'That's very true,' she agreed. 'Now, let's get all these plants safely into the minibus, which is going to be a job and a half. Then I reckon we all deserve a cup of tea in the garden centre café.'

She didn't *just* mean a cup of tea. She let Selma and me choose any cake we wanted too. This took quite a time because there were great big gateaux with whirly cream and cherries on top, and huge golden slices of jam sponge cake, and enormous slabs of chocolate cake with frosting, not to mention scones and brownies and cookies the size of plates.

In the end, after much deliberation, we had twin slices of gateau, the last two on the plate.

'Phil and Maddie and I nearly always choose the same cake. Good job it's just us two today,' I said to Selma.

'Bet you can't eat all that cake, though. You've got such a titchy appetite,' said Selma.

'You watch me,' I said. I ate it all up, every crumb, every dab of whirly cream, every cherry.

Miss Lovejoy just nibbled on a boring old scone. She didn't even have jam and cream, just butter.

'You didn't want a slice of the gateau too, did you, Miss Lovejoy?' I asked, suddenly worried.

'No, dear, I'm very much a scone person.' Miss Lovejoy smiled. 'Plain and no nonsense and old-fashioned.'

'I think you're really lovely,' I said shyly. 'You've been sooooo kind. Hasn't she, Selma?'

'Yeah, you've been great, miss,' said Selma.

'Miss *Lovejoy*,' said Miss Lovejoy, but she was still smiling.

Chapter Twenty-Two

That evening I spent ages making a plan for the butterfly garden. I remembered each and every plant so I could sketch out the way they'd look prettiest. I decided to have a buddleia at either end, and then masses of flowers in-between.

The next day Selma brought in two big carrier bags full of nettles and dandelions, each with their own clod of earth to protect their roots.

'I wore gloves so them nettles didn't sting me,' she said proudly.

Miss Lovejoy parked the minibus by the garden strip and started unloading all our flowers and shrubs.

We were so busy planting at lunch time! We needed to get all the plants settled really quickly, so Miss Lovejoy suggested we ask for help. Phil and Neera and Maddie and Harry came to ease the plants out of their containers, while Miss Lovejoy and Selma and I dug holes and put each one in place. Then we moved on to the next and the next while the others watered them in, using a great big watering can. Harry was the chief waterer and managed to water himself as much as the plants.

It was a bit annoying, because Selma and I would have loved to do some watering too.

'But you two are the expert gardeners now,' said Miss Lovejoy. 'You need to make sure the plants are at the right depth, with their roots able to spread out comfortably. And don't worry, you'll need to do lots more work watering to help them grow.'

The three of us had to work together to cope

with the big buddleia bushes. One simply wouldn't come out of its container and we had to tug and heave. But eventually it shifted.

We weren't anywhere near finished when the bell rang for afternoon school, but Miss Lovejoy gave Selma and me special permission to miss drama and games so we could carry on with the planting and sow the cabbages and beans.

We worked and worked and worked, and got everything finished five minutes before the bell went for home time. We gave everything another watering – Selma had to help me when it was my turn because the can was so heavy. Then we just stood hand in hand and looked at the garden.

It didn't look *quite* as pretty as my picture. Miss Lovejoy said we had to space things out a bit to give the plants room to grow and spread, so there were gaps of brown earth everywhere. But even so it still looked a splendid garden.

I threw back my head. 'Come on, butterflies! Come to our garden!' I called enticingly.

But they didn't come.

Oh dear, they didn't come.

They didn't come.

Selma and I went to the butterfly garden every day and waited. We looked until our eyes watered, but we didn't see a single butterfly.

'It's because it's not warm enough yet,' said Selma. 'It's only March, for goodness' sake.'

'My butterfly book says the big nymph butterflies – the painted lady and the peacock and the red admiral, all the *best* butterflies – start flying around in March,'

I said mournfully. 'They must be flying around right this minute. But in other people's gardens. Not ours.'

'You've got to give them a chance, Little Bug. They'll come soon,' said Selma.

'I'm giving them lots of chances, Big Bug. But nothing's happening,' I said.

'Didn't you say some of them like rotting fruit? Pretty weird of them, I must say, but still, let's try it. Your mum's always giving you lots of fruit for your lunch. Let's scatter it about the garden and see if it will make the butterflies come,' Selma suggested.

So I didn't eat my apples or clementines for a whole week. We cut them into quarters and left them in the garden.

But the butterflies still didn't come.

'All that work! All that money!' I said, nearly in tears.

'But we've still got a lovely garden,' said Selma.

'I don't like it now,' I said. 'It's pointless if it doesn't work. I'm not going to go there any more.'

'Oh, don't be silly. You don't really mean that.'

'Yes I do,' I said.

I wouldn't go to the butterfly garden that playtime. I didn't go at lunch time either.

'I'll still go,' said Selma. 'Just to have a look.'

She dashed off every time the bell went. She shook her head whenever she came back. 'Sorry. Didn't see any. But they *will* come, I just know they will.'

She went to accost Miss Lovejoy. 'We will get some butterflies coming to our garden, won't we, miss?'

'Miss *Lovejoy*. Yes, I'm sure you will. It will just take a little time, that's all. The butterflies have to find the garden. Once they start coming, then they'll mate and lay eggs, and the caterpillars will feed there and pupate and then hatch out into more butterflies, and in a year or so I'm sure you'll see butterflies there every day,' she said.

'A *year*?' I said. 'I want to see butterflies there *now*!'

'One of the most important lessons to learn in life is patience,' said Miss Lovejoy.

I might have learned how to spell *patience*

333

now, but I didn't have any. And Miss Lovejoy was starting to get on my nerves.

Selma seemed surprisingly pally with her nowadays. She went up to her at the end of school and went *whisper whisper whisper*. Miss Lovejoy beckoned her to the store cupboard and gave her a whole lot of different-coloured sugar paper, which Selma folded carefully and then crammed into her school bag.

'What have you got all that paper for?' I asked.

Selma gently tweaked my nose. 'Nosy! You wait and see,' she said.

At playtime the next day Selma ran off and didn't come back. I was stuck all by myself, sitting on the steps by the library. I looked for Phil, but she was playing some sort of silly game with Neera. I looked for Maddie, but she was playing football with Harry. It was very lonely without Selma. I wondered about going to the butterfly garden after all, but I couldn't bear to now.

Then, just as the bell went, Selma came running. 'Quick! Quick, Tina! Come to the garden!' she yelled.

'Have you seen a butterfly?' I gasped.

'Heaps!' said Selma, tugging at my hands. 'Quick! Come and see them.'

I ran like the wind, all the way over to the butterfly garden. Then I stood still, transfixed. There were at least twenty butterflies all over the flowers and shrubs. Not real ones. These were paper butterflies – blue and brown and pink and green and white, all carefully cut out and sellotaped to the leaves.

'Oh my goodness!' I said.

'I did it just so you can see what it will look like,' said Selma. 'Do you like them?'

'Oh, Selma, they look lovely, truly lovely,' I said. 'Tell you what – let's form a club, you and me. The Butterfly Club.'

'With just two members?' said Selma. 'That would be cool. And I've found someone to cheer you up. Look carefully!'

I looked and looked. And then I saw a tiny little person carefully taped to a lavender bush. A small china person.

'Baby!' I breathed.

Selma carefully detached her and put her in my hand.

'Oh, Baby, I've got you back at last!' I said, clutching her tight and starting to cry.

'She got lost for a while,' Selma said, not quite looking at me, 'and then I found her. I wanted to keep her, but I knew she was really yours. You've been so miserable and you needed her.'

'Oh, Selma, thank you so much!' I said.

'Well, that's what friends are for, isn't it?' she said.

'You're the best friend in all the world!'

'Really? We're best friends now? You really mean it?'

'Yes, I really mean it. And tell you what – you can have New Baby. She's bigger than this baby and she's got proper clothes. You'll like her, I promise.'

'So are you a bit happier now? You're still crying!'

'Only a bit.'

'You don't mind so much that there aren't any butterflies yet?'

'Well, we've got paper butterflies, haven't we?'

'They're not very good. Some of their wings

347

went wonky and they're not really the right colours. I'm not brilliant at art like you.'

'I think they're beautiful,' I declared. 'Lovely, lovely butterflies!'

And then, as I spoke, a real butterfly came flying through the air. A real, wonderful butterfly, with red wings and blue spots like eyes.

A peacock! I mouthed at Selma, not daring to speak aloud.

It circled all the way round the garden, alighted on one of the purple buddleia sprays, and fluttered its wings. It stayed there for several seconds and then flew away.

'It *was* real, wasn't it?' I whispered, scared that I might have imagined it.

'It was totally real,' said Selma. 'I bet it came because it saw all my paper butterflies. They acted like a signal to it. *Come here, you guys*, it said. *Lots of nectar going free!*'

'You did it, Selma! You're magic. Let's see if the peacock butterfly comes back – or maybe there'll be others!'

But we didn't get a chance to see that day, because Kayleigh came running towards us, bright red in the face with triumph.

'You two, Selma and Tina! You're in soooo much trouble! Miss Lovejoy sent me looking for you. You're ten minutes late for lessons. Ha ha, serves you both right! Miss Lovejoy will kill you!'

'You shut up, Kayleigh,' Selma said fiercely.

'No I won't! What have you been doing, anyway? Just staring at your silly garden? What are all them paper things? They look silly!'

'No they don't! They're brilliant,' I said fiercely. 'They made a real peacock butterfly come.'

'Rubbish,' said Kayleigh.

'It's not not not rubbish! We saw it, didn't we, Selma?'

'Yeah, we saw it and that's all that matters. We don't care if we get into trouble with Miss Lovejoy,' said Selma.

But we *didn't* get into trouble. Miss Lovejoy was looking very fierce when we went into the classroom, but when she saw our faces she actually smiled.

'Did you like Selma's paper butterflies, Tina?' she asked.

'Yes, they're lovely, and they worked like magic – because guess what, Miss Lovejoy, we saw a peacock butterfly – we really did, didn't we, Selma?'

'You bet we did! It was on one of them buddleia bushes, miss!' said Selma.

'Miss *Lovejoy*!' said Miss Lovejoy. 'Well, you're very naughty girls not to come back into school the moment the bell rang, and I shall make you stay an extra ten minutes after lessons have ended – but all the same, how splendid! A peacock butterfly, eh! So the butterfly garden has had its first visitor at last!'

Chapter Twenty-Three

More butterflies came! A painted lady, a red admiral, a brimstone, a large white, and many more. Selma and I ticked them off triumphantly in the butterfly book.

We left Selma's paper butterflies in place. When it was breezy their wings fluttered as if they were real. But then, one night, there was a storm, and when we went to look the next day the paper butterflies were all in sodden shreds, so we had to remove them. I dried the biggest out carefully and then tucked it inside the butterfly book as a keepsake. I showed Selma and she was very pleased.

We sat beside the butterfly garden every day. Phil and Neera and Maddie and Harry and lots of the other children came to watch the butterflies too. It was wonderful to show off and identify the butterflies for them. Alistair was a bit annoying because *he* got a butterfly book too, and started dividing butterflies into families – the small skippers, large swallowtails and pale whites; the small bright hairstreaks, coppers and blues; and the glorious nymphs. He even tried to learn their Latin names. He knelt at the edge of the garden, spouting butterfly information for all he was worth.

'Shut up, Alistair!' said Selma. 'It's *our* butterfly garden, me and Tina's, not yours. *We* made it. And we don't want to hear you spouting all this stuff. Tina's the one who knows about butterflies, not you.'

'Yes, but—'

'*No* but! You're doing my head in. We just want to sit peacefully and watch,' said Selma.

'OK, OK, keep your hair on. I'll watch too,' he said.

He sat quietly – but we could see his lips moving as he whispered informatively to himself.

When Miss Lovejoy was on playground duty she came and watched as well. So did some of the other teachers.

'It's worked a treat,' said Mr Haringay, who teaches Year Six. 'All that hard work digging has paid off at last. My goodness, those little girls slaved away day after day. I wonder why you didn't take up my offer of hiring a rotavator? The whole area could have been dug over in no time.'

'Yes, I wonder why,' said Miss Lovejoy, smiling mysteriously.

'Still, they've done a grand job.'

'They have indeed.'

I took my coloured pencils and sketchpad to school and drew lots of pictures of the butterfly garden.

'Draw us sitting beside it,' said Selma, so I did.

I missed looking at the garden during the

summer half term. I drew more pictures at home with Phil and Maddie. We also started up a new club – a triplet one just for us. We had to say everything three times, and we made lists of our three favourite foods, three favourite animals, three favourite colours, three favourite television shows, three favourite hobbies, three favourite books, three favourite people at school, three favourite songs, three favourite sports, three favourite butterflies . . . Guess who chose the last category!

When it was sunny we played football-in-slow-motion. This was a soft, gentle version so that Mum wouldn't get fussed about me playing. Grandad looked after us while Mum and Dad were working, and he played football-in-slo-mo too. He still got a bit puffed, much more than me.

Sometimes we left Phil and Maddie playing kickabout and went and sat on the sofa and watched television for ten minutes to catch our breath. Grandad didn't mind a bit watching *Ruby Red* on CBeebies. He chuckled at Ruby too and joined in all her games. He liked looking at all the children's drawings at the end of the show.

'You should send one of your pictures in, Tina,' he said.

'I'm too old, Grandad! This is a programme for little kids,' I told him.

'You're just a little squirt yourself, you soppy ha'porth! I don't think there's an age limit anyway.' He squinted at the television screen. 'There, look! That boy's picture of a fire engine – it says *By Matthew, aged seven*. See! You're only seven, Tina. Go on, have a go. Your pictures are much better than that.'

'Do you really think so? Oh goodness, what if Ruby picked mine! Which one shall I send?' I asked, getting excited.

Grandad looked at all the pictures in my sketchbook, peering at each one carefully. 'I think I'd choose this one,' he said, stopping at the picture of Selma and me in the butterfly garden.

So I tore it out of the pad very carefully. I printed my name and address on the back – and then I added a little piece to explain my picture.

The girls in this picture are my best friend Selma and me. We made this butterfly garden at school. We dug the earth for ages and put compost down and raised money and bought lots of plants and NOW lots of butterflies come to have a drink of nectar in our garden.

I was a much better speller nowadays, but I checked all the dodgy words with Grandad just to make sure it was all perfect. Grandad said he would find a big stiff envelope so that my drawing wouldn't get crumpled, and then he'd post it off for me.

A week later, when I was back at school, I got a letter.

'A letter just for me!' I said when I found it waiting for me at home.

I'd never ever had my own letter before. Gran and Grandad often sent postcards when they were on holiday, but they were always addressed to Phil and Maddie and me.

'Let me see!' said Mum.

'Hey, let Tina open it,' said Dad. 'It's her letter.'

So I opened it and stared hard at the type-written message inside.

Dear Tina,

We simply loved your picture of
the butterfly garden. Would you
and Selma like to come on the
programme and talk to Ruby Red
about it? Talk it over with your
parents or guardians, and if
they think this is a good idea
ask them to telephone us on the

```
number at the top of the page.
With all good wishes,
```

Garnet Baker

```
Garnet Baker
Executive Producer,
the Ruby Red team
```

I read it through twice, unable to believe it.

'What does it *say*?' asked Phil.

'Shall we read it for you?' said Maddie.

'I can read it myself,' I said, my voice all wobbly.

'Oh darling, what is it? Give it here,' said Mum.

I handed it over and she read it through quickly, Dad peering over her shoulder. 'Oh my goodness!' she said.

'What?' said Phil.

'*What?*' said Maddie.

'Our Tina's going on television!' said Dad, and he picked me up and whirled me round and round.

'But when did you send this picture to the programme?' Mum asked, bewildered.

'Grandad sent it,' I said.

'Well, good for him!' said Dad.

Phil and Maddie were looking at the letter now.

'Oh, Tina, you lucky thing!' said Phil.

'I've always wanted to be on television,' said Maddie.

'I'll mention you two when I phone up,' said Mum. 'You're triplets – you always do things together – and you'll be a novelty item on the programme. I don't see why Selma has to come. I'm sure her mum will create difficulties anyway. It will be so much better, the three of you. Maybe we could buy you identical butterfly T-shirts – that would be really eye-catching!'

'Hey, hey, hey,' said Dad. 'Don't get too carried away, love. We can't do Selma out of her chance to be on the telly.'

'No we can't,' I said, loudly and firmly. 'If it wasn't for Selma there wouldn't be any butterfly garden. She did practically one hundred per cent of the hard work – all that digging!'

'You sound like Alistair!' said Maddie.

'Yes, but I suppose it's true,' said Phil.

'And maybe if she hadn't tied all the paper butterflies to the plants, the real ones wouldn't have come too. Selma *has* to come with me. Besides, she's my best friend,' I said.

Mum sighed. 'I don't know why you're so keen on her. I feel sorry for her myself, but she's the same little girl who used to be so nasty to you, and stole your china dolly.'

'She didn't steal Baby, she only borrowed her, and now I've got her back,' I said, taking Baby out of my pocket and waving her about.

'So you'd sooner go on television with Selma than with Phil and me?' asked Maddie.

'I wouldn't *sooner*, exactly – but it's only fair that I do,' I said.

'Yes, but won't you need us to do some of the talking for you?' said Phil. 'What if you have to read something out? You know you need us when you get nervous.'

'I won't be nervous. I want to meet Ruby Red. And I like talking about butterflies and my garden,' I said.

As it turned out, I felt very, very nervous all the way to the studio. The television people sent a big car to take us there. It was a good job it was big because there were a lot of people squashed inside. There was Mum. There was Selma. Selma's mum said she couldn't come, but nobody minded, not even Selma. There was me. I didn't take up too much room, so Mum said Phil and Maddie could come too, just to watch. She'd bought us matching butterfly T-shirts all the same. Phil's was pink, Maddie's was blue and mine was green. She bought one for Selma too – a red one.

'You look really nice in it, lovey,' Mum said when Selma put it on.

Selma just shrugged and didn't say thank you properly, but I could tell she was really pleased.

'I'm glad mine's red,' she said, and she kept stroking the soft new T-shirt material.

She was wearing her friendship bracelet, and that had red beads too, so she matched. She had New Baby in her jeans pocket. I had my dear old Baby in mine. I soon fished her out and clutched her tight for comfort.

It was quite a long way to the studio and the traffic was very bad, so we kept stopping and starting. I already had a weird feeling in my tummy. The feeling got worse and worse, until I was scared I was going to be sick.

'Aren't you feeling well, Tina?' Mum asked anxiously.

'I'm fine,' I said in a tiny voice.

I was squashed between Selma and Phil and couldn't really move. What if I was sick all over them?

The driver looked a little like Grandad. He peered at me in his rear-view mirror, and then pressed a button to wind down the windows. 'Let's have a little air in the car,' he said. 'We'll blow those cobwebs away.'

It felt a bit better in the breeze, but the wobbling in my tummy was still bad. I kept fidgeting.

'Are you *sure* you're all right, Tina?' Phil hissed.

I nodded.

She and Maddie started playing a game of I Spy. I didn't join in. Neither did Selma.

'What's up?' she whispered in my ear.

'My tummy feels all fluttery and weird,' I whispered back.

Selma paused. Then she grinned. 'You've got butterflies in your tummy!' she said.

I couldn't help bursting out laughing. I felt quite a bit better then, though the weird feeling didn't go away. I started rubbing my tummy, muttering, 'Painted lady, peacock, brimstone, Adonis blue . . .' picturing them all, adding exotic butterflies from overseas too – 'green swallowtail, blue morpho, postman . . .' – imagining them all fluttering together in my tummy and then swirling up, escaping out of my mouth and flying around the car, out of the open window, and up into the blue sky above.

Then we got to the studios and the weird feeling got worse and worse. I hung onto Selma's hand. Even Phil and Maddie looked a little worried, and they didn't even have to do anything.

'Look out for famous people!' said Maddie as we went inside.

'Our Tina's going to be a little bit famous!' said Phil. 'Imagine!'

We had to announce our names to the receptionist, and then we were all given special name badges to wear around our necks – even Mum and Phil and Maddie. Then we had to wait on a big sofa for someone to collect us.

It was a girl in amazing rainbow boots.

'Hi, everyone. Mrs Maynard? And let me guess – Tina? And you must be Selma. And, oh my goodness, twins!'

'Triplets actually,' said Phil.

'We're Tina's sisters. I'm Maddie, she's Phil.'

'Wonderful!' said the rainbow girl. 'Well, come with me, folks, and I'll take you upstairs.'

'Did you write the letter? Are you Garnet Baker?' Mum asked.

'No, no, you'll meet her in a minute. I'm Jane, I'm just the runner,' she said.

'Wow, can you get a job in the studios as a runner?' said Maddie. 'I'd like to do that. How far do you have to run?'

'I don't really have to *run*. I just whiz up and down the corridors collecting people and going for coffees and taking people to their dressing rooms and just generally making myself useful,' said Jane.

'That would be brilliant!' said Maddie, her eyes shining.

'Is Tina going to have her own dressing room?' asked Phil.

'She's dressed already. I bought those butterfly T-shirts specially,' said Mum.

'"Dressing room" is just a figure of speech,' said Jane. 'It's just a private room where you can all hang out until we need you in the studio. Tina and Selma might have to pop along to make-up first.'

'Make-up!' said Phil. 'Oh, you lucky things!'

'I hope that's another figure of speech,' said Mum. 'They're much too young to wear make-up!'

'I'm not,' said Selma quickly. 'I'm much bigger than Tina. *I* want to wear make-up.'

'It's not a proper full make-up. Just a little powder to stop the girls looking shiny under the studio lights,' said Jane.

She led us in and out of lifts and along many corridors, and at last we came to several dressing-room doors. To my astonishment, the nearest door had a placard saying

```
TINA MAYNARD AND
SELMA JOHNSON
```

'Oh my!' said Maddie. 'See, you're famous already!'

The dressing room wasn't particularly grand inside – it was just a small room with an oldish sofa and chair and a big mirror.

'Would you like a coffee, Mrs Maynard?' Jane

offered. 'And what would you girls like? Coke or orange juice?'

'Coke!' we all chorused.

'Orange juice,' said Mum firmly.

Jane laughed, and when she brought a tray of drinks five minutes later there were little cartons of orange *and* four cans  of Coke. 'So you can choose,' she said. 'Well, I'd better pop back to the studio now. Garnet will be along in a minute to talk you through the show. Enjoy yourselves!'

I still had a host of butterflies in my tummy but I was starting to enjoy myself. I was just taking a long slug of Coke when the door opened and someone very familiar walked in. I was so surprised I forgot to swallow and the Coke spurted down my T-shirt.

'Oh, Tina!' said Mum, dabbing at me with a tissue. 'All over your new T-shirt!'

'It's Ruby!' I spluttered, awestruck.

She looked slightly different. She didn't

have her mad pigtails with the red ribbons and she wasn't wearing her red-and-white striped T-shirt or her red dungarees. She'd cut her hair to shoulder length and she was wearing black jeans and a black T-shirt – but I'd have known her anywhere.

But I was wrong!

'Are you OK, Tina? Sorry to give you a fright! Actually I'm not Ruby – I'm Garnet,' she said.

We all stared.

'But you do look ever so like Ruby Red!' said Phil.

'I know. So why do you think that is?' Garnet looked at Phil and Maddie. 'You two girls should guess straight away!'

'Oh my goodness – are you Ruby Red's twin?' asked Maddie.

'That's right. We used to look like two peas in a pod when we were little, before we started to dress differently,' said Garnet. 'Just like you!'

'We're not actually twins, though,' said Phil.

'We're triplets, Maddie and Tina and me.'

'But I'm the one who's different,' I said.

'You're the one who knows all about butterflies,' said Garnet, smiling. 'And you must be Selma, Tina's friend.'

'I'm her best friend,' said Selma. 'And I did nearly all the digging because I'm the strongest.'

'I brought Phil and Maddie along because I thought you'd be interested to see the triplets – they're a bit of a novelty item,' said Mum. 'And they're all in the same class at school so they were involved with the butterfly garden too.'

'No they weren't!' said Selma. She sounded rude, but I knew she was scared of being left out.

Mum smiled stiffly. 'Now then, Selma!' she said.

'Selma did the most,' I said quickly.

'I'm sure we can use *all* the girls,' said Garnet. 'I'll just amend the script a little.' She started scribbling on the papers she was holding.

'Have we got to learn lines?' Selma asked, looking worried.

'No, no, there's just an outline of the way the scene will go,' said Garnet.

'Won't the scriptwriter mind you changing it?' asked Phil.

Garnet laughed. '*I'm* the scriptwriter as well as the producer,' she said.

'So does Ruby Red have to do what you say?' I wondered.

'She's supposed to – but that doesn't mean she does!' said Garnet. 'You girls know what sisters can be like.'

Phil and Maddie and I all nodded vigorously.

'Now, I'll take all four of you to make-up and then we'll go to the studio. Ruby's already there,' said Garnet.

The make-up lady was called Moira. We took turns sitting in the chair with an overall round our neck while she dabbed powder on our noses and combed our hair. Selma begged for a little lipstick, so Moira selected a pale pink pearly one that hardly showed. Then Phil and Maddie wanted it too. And me.

'Dear me, you're demanding little ladies,' said Moira, but she was only teasing us.

Then Garnet took us to the studio. It was a

confusing room – very dark in places, with all sorts of wires and leads you could trip over, and then very bright at the end, where the cameras were. There was Ruby Red's playroom, with her squashy red sofa and her shiny red table and her red play box full of paper and crayons and scissors – and there was Ruby Red herself!

The butterflies in my tummy fluttered again. It was so strange seeing Ruby in real life, in her familiar red outfit, with her funny plaits, when I was so used to seeing her little on the television. But she smiled as soon as she saw us.

'Hi, you guys!' she said, dashing up to us. 'I'm Ruby. So I'm guessing you're Tina, our butterfly-garden girl?'

'Yes, and these are my sisters Phil and Maddie, and this is my friend Selma,' I said shyly.

'I'm her best friend,' said Selma. 'And I did nearly all the digging for the garden.'

'Yep, I can see you're the girl with muscles!' said Ruby, squeezing Selma's arms and looking impressed.

Selma smiled proudly.

'Well, I'm going to chat to you all, and we'll show your beautiful picture, Tina, and then you can tell us about making the butterfly garden,' said Ruby. 'Let's pop a little microphone on all of you.'

A nice man attached a baby microphone to the tops of our T-shirts and we tucked the battery case into our jeans pockets.

Selma peered around at the cameras, waving at each one. 'Can people at home see me waving?' she asked.

'No, not yet. This is just a recording – we're not going out live. And try not to look at the cameras. Just look at me,' said Ruby.

'Right, shall we get started?' said Garnet. 'Tina, come and stand beside Ruby. Selma and Phil and Maddie, you sit on the sofa, OK?'

'Good luck, girls!' said Mum. 'Don't be scared, Tina. Try to smile!'

But all of a sudden I was very, very, very scared. I thought of all the thousands and thousands of children who would be watching *Ruby Red*. They might all be pointing at me, saying, *Look at that stupid titchy girl and her boring picture!*

The butterflies swarmed in my stomach. 'Please, I think I might be sick!' I squeaked.

'Oh dear, oh dear,' said Mum. 'I'll take her.'

She whisked me out of the studio and along the corridor to the ladies' room. She rushed me into a cubicle and held my head. Even though I felt very sick, nothing happened. I went to the loo instead, but when I got a bit tangled with the microphone lead I wondered if everyone in the studio might have heard me weeing.

I burst into tears.

'Oh, Tina!' said Mum. 'Come here and have a cuddle. Don't worry, darling. You don't have to do this if you really don't want to. I'm sure Phil and Maddie could talk about the butterfly garden instead. You can just hold your pretty picture up. How about that?'

I cried harder.

'Oh dear, you poor pet. I *thought* this might happen,' said Mum.

Then Garnet came into the ladies. I hid my face, horribly embarrassed.

'Don't worry, Tina,' she said gently. 'I know exactly how you feel.' She gave me a big clean tissue and I mopped at my face.

'When Ruby and I were young we went to an audition to play twins in a children's television serial. Ruby desperately wanted us to get the parts. She's always wanted to be an actress. I was so shy and awkward I couldn't say a word.'

'Really?' I said, sniffing.

'Yes, really. I was used to Ruby saying everything for me.'

'Yes, well, that's what I think we ought to do,' said Mum. 'Phil and Maddie can say stuff – they're not a bit shy. Then Tina might feel able to join in a bit.'

'But the butterfly garden was all *your* idea, wasn't it, Tina? And *you* made it all,' said Garnet.

'With Selma,' I said.

'Yes, with Selma. So I think it would be lovely if you could be brave enough to tell us all about it. Remember, it's just a recording. If you suddenly get your words mixed up we can stop and start again.'

'I don't like the thought of all the people watching me,' I said, blowing my nose.

'I know, but we're going to try to forget about them. It'll just be you and your friend and your sisters and Ruby having a little chat. Do you think you can give it a go? I'd really, really like it if you could, because I think this is going to be one of our best programmes ever. It will be wonderful if we can encourage other children to make their own butterfly gardens,' said Garnet.

I had a sudden picture in my head of hundreds

of new gardens all over the country, with swarms of butterflies flying over each. It was such a lovely thought that I couldn't help smiling.

'There!' said Garnet. 'Good girl. We'd better whisk you back to make-up to powder that sniffly red nose and then we'll give it a go, OK?'

'OK,' I said.

And it *was* OK.

I knew that Phil and Maddie wouldn't tease me when I got back to the studio, but I was worried about Selma.

I didn't need to be.

'Are you all right, Tina?' she asked anxiously. 'Were you really sick?'

'No, I just felt it.'

'Well, hold Baby tight. She'll make you feel better. You can hold New Baby too if you like, for extra comfort,' she offered.

'No, I'm fine now, I think. But thank you,' I said, and I squeezed her hand instead of Baby's.

Then we started filming.

'Hi. I'm Ruby Red and this is my bright red room,' said Ruby. 'Here's my bright red table and

my bright red chair and my bright red play box
– and look who's sitting on my bright red sofa!

'One, two, three, *four* girls come to say hello. Now,
I *know* this is Tina, because she sent me the most
beautiful picture. Come and tell me who the other
girls are, Tina.'

'These are my sisters, Phil and Maddie,' I said,
and they each gave me a little wave.

'Hello, Phil. Hello, Maddie. My goodness, you look absolutely identical. So you're twins?' asked Ruby.

'No, we're triplets,' said Phil.

'Tina's a triplet too but she's a bit smaller than us,' Maddie explained.

'I'm getting a bit bigger now,' I said.

'She's still much littler than me!' Selma pointed out.

'This is Selma, my best friend,' I said.

'And we made the butterfly garden together. I did all the digging!' said Selma.

'Yes, you're the strongest girl,' said Ruby. 'I think you're probably stronger than me, Selma. But it was you who first got interested in butterflies, wasn't it, Tina?'

'I liked drawing them. Miss Lovejoy gave me a book about butterflies when I was ill,' I said.

'And who's Miss Lovejoy?' Ruby asked.

'She's our teacher,' said Selma.

'Is she a nice teacher?'

'She's a very *good* teacher, but she's very strict,' said Phil.

'She can be really scary at times,' added Maddie. 'Even our mum is a bit scared of her!'

There was a little squeak of protest from the corner of the studio where Mum was watching.

'I'm not scared of her. I like her,' said Selma unexpectedly.

'I like her too. She's very kind,' I said. 'She helped us raise money for a butterfly garden and bought all the plants with us. And she paid me heaps when I did a sponsored spelling test!'

'Are you good at spelling, Tina?'

'I didn't use to be. But maybe I am now!'

'And you're certainly very, very good at drawing pictures. Here's your butterfly garden picture. Would you like to hold it up and show everyone?'

I held up my picture. I knew the camera was pointing at it.

'Here's me, and here's Selma. And these are all the plants that butterflies like. Buddleia – they like that best. Some people actually call it the "butterfly bush". And primula, aubretia, bugle, sweet william, lavender, red valerian and asters.

369

They've all got lots and lots of nectar,' I said, pointing to each plant in turn.

'And dandelions and nettles – they like them too. I found them for nothing,' said Selma. 'We're the Butterfly Club, Tina and me. Just us!'

'And there are all the butterflies, flying around your garden,' said Ruby.

'There are the real butterflies – a peacock, a red admiral, a brimstone, an Adonis blue – although that's cheating because our garden isn't chalky enough – and these here are paper butterflies. Selma tied them to the bushes to cheer me up when the real butterflies took a long time coming,' I said.

'Well, I think it's absolutely beautiful,' said Ruby. 'I'm going to try to make a butterfly garden too.'

She looked at the camera. 'Why don't you ask a grown-up if you can make a little patch of garden specially for butterflies! If you go to the *Ruby Red* website you'll find a list of all the plants that butterflies particularly like. It's time to say goodbye now. Wave goodbye to everyone, Tina and Selma and Phil and Maddie. Goodbye, goodbye!'

'Goodbye!' we all chorused, and we waved too.

'Keep waving!' Ruby muttered, so we waved and waved.

'There!' she said at last. 'Well done!'

'That was brilliant!' said Garnet. 'You were all absolutely perfect. I'm so proud of you all. Didn't they do well, Mrs Maynard? *Especially* Tina!'

'You spoke up beautifully, darling! Who would ever have thought it?' said Mum.

'She's a natural,' said Ruby. 'Don't you think so, Garnet?'

'I certainly do,' said Garnet. 'Perhaps you'll be a television star one day, Tina! Would you like that?'

They were so kind to me, but perhaps they didn't really mean it. And I don't really want to be a television star when I'm older. I want to study butterflies.

When we're grown up Phil and Maddie and I want to live in the same house together so we

371

can still be Phil and Maddie and me. If we all earn lots of money, perhaps it can be quite a big house with four bedrooms. Then we can be Phil and Maddie and me – and Selma.

Take Tina's Test!

Now that you've read Tina's story, test yourself! How many of these questions can you answer?

1. Who gave Tina her precious doll, Baby?

2. Can you name the sisters' hamsters, which they buy with their birthday money from Grandad?

3. Selma nicknames Tina 'Little Bug'. What nickname does she give to Phil and Maddie, which Tina thinks is very unfair?

4. Selma scribbles out a drawing that Tina is very proud of – what is it?

5. When Gran and Grandad take the girls to the zoo, what does Tina say is her favourite butterfly?

6. How many spellings does Miss Lovejoy ask Tina to learn for her spelling challenge?

7. Miss Lovejoy tells Tina that she is planning a trip to an exciting faraway destination, and Tina draws her a picture of that place as a present – where is it?

8. When Tina visits Selma's home, what do they eat?

9. What's the first real butterfly to visit Tina and Selma's butterfly garden?

10. Ruby Red and her sister Garnet appeared in another brilliant book by Jacqueline Wilson! Can you name it?

The Life Cycle of a Butterfly

Tina and the rest of Miss Lovejoy's class learn all about the life cycle of butterflies. How much do you know about them, and the different stages of their lives?

STAGE ONE: THE EGG

The butterfly lays her eggs on a leaf or a stem, where they will stick, so that they won't blow off in the wind or rain. These eggs can be round, oval or even cylindrical, depending on what kind of butterfly laid them. If you were able to look very closely at an egg, you might actually be able to see the tiny caterpillar growing inside it!

STAGE TWO: THE CATERPILLAR

These are also known as 'larvae', and are often patterned with stripes. Caterpillars are very tiny when they first hatch, but grow quickly.

The most important thing a caterpillar can do is eat! In fact, the first thing a new caterpillar will do when it emerges is munch through the leaf it was born on. You might have seen caterpillars chomping through leaves in your garden!

STAGE THREE: THE CHRYSALIS
Another name for this is the 'pupa'. This is where the caterpillar spins a cocoon around itself made from a very special silk. Once inside this cocoon, the caterpillar transforms into the very final stage of its life cycle.

STAGE FOUR: THE BEAUTIFUL BUTTERFLY!
If you're ever lucky enough to see a brand-new butterfly emerging from its cocoon, you will notice that it doesn't open up its wings immediately.

This is because they have been wrapped tightly against its body for so long, and need to open up slowly so that blood can flow into them. But within a few hours, a butterfly will start to flap its wings and fly. Then it's time for the butterfly to look for a mate – and the cycle will start all over again!

All About Butterflies!

If, like Tina, you'd like to know more about butterflies, here are a few interesting facts to get you started:

☆ Butterflies have taste receptors on a very unusual part of their body . . . their feet!

☆ No one knows for sure how many different types of butterfly there are in the world, but it's thought to be as many as 20,000.

☆ The smallest butterfly is just an eighth of an inch long – that's this tiny:

☆ The longest is around 12 inches long. That's twice the width of this book!

☆ Pictures of butterflies were found in ancient Egyptian wall paintings that are over 3,000 years old. Butterflies have been around for a long, long time!

☆ Butterflies actually have their skeletons on the *outside* of their bodies. This is called an exoskeleton, and it protects the most fragile parts of the butterfly.

☆ Monarch butterflies are known to migrate thousands of miles every winter, heading for warmer climates

☆ The Italian word for butterfly is 'farfalla' – which is also the word for a bow-tie, and a type of pasta that has a very similar shape.

☆ Butterflies have some of the prettiest names in the natural world. Phil, Maddie and Tina pick the emerald swallowtail, the blue Adonis, and the postman as their special favourites, but some others you might like to look up are the silver-spotted skipper, the mountain ringlet, the clouded yellow, the purple emperor, the American painted lady, the geranium bronze and the crimson rose.

Create Your Own Butterfly Garden

If you feel inspired to build your own butterfly garden like Tina and Selma, here are a few tips to get you started. Remember to ask a parent or teacher for permission and help.

First of all, pick a corner of your garden or school playing field that is sheltered from the wind. Butterflies are delicate creatures with fragile wings that can tear in strong wind, so an area surrounded by a fence or hedge is a good idea. If you can, try to avoid somewhere that might be popular with cats and dogs too!

Start with a layer of good quality soil, well-raked.
Then it's time to start planting!

The most important thing in a butterfly garden is –
flowers! And the wider the variety of flowers, the better.
Flowers produce nectar, which is food for butterflies,
and different types of butterflies are attracted to
different types of nectar – so the more different
kinds of flowers you make available, the more
butterflies you'll see fluttering around your garden.

Try to pick plants and flowers that will bloom at
different times throughout the year. This will en-
sure that your butterflies will always have food,
no matter the season. It's especially important
that there are lots of flowers blooming during
the summer months, as that's
when butterflies are
usually most active.

Aster, purple coneflowers, milkweed (sometimes known as butterfly weed!) and lilac will supply nectar for several years – these are called 'perennials'. Other good choices are marigolds and petunias, which are 'annuals' – this means they will only live for one year, and will then need replacing.

It's also really important that your garden gets lots of sunlight, because butterflies don't produce their own body heat like we do, and so they need to rest in the sun as much as possible. It's also key that there are plenty of leafy green plants – not just flowers – so that your butterflies have somewhere to lay their eggs, and caterpillars have lots to munch on.

If you'd like to share pictures of your butterfly garden with other fans of Jacqueline's books, visit **www.jacquelinewilson.co.uk**.

Maddie and Phil's Puzzle Page!

Can you spot the ten differences between these two pictures?

Make Tina and Selma's Butterfly Cakes!

You might want to ask an adult to help you make these delicious cakes.

INGREDIENTS:
115g soft butter
115g caster sugar
115g self raising flour
2 medium eggs
1 teaspoon vanilla essence

FOR THE TOPPING:
55g soft butter
115g icing sugar

1. First, preheat the oven to 190°C.

2. Mix the butter and sugar together until you have a light, fluffy, creamy mixture.

3. Beat the eggs, then add them to your creamy mixture very gradually, along with the flour. Then add the vanilla.

4. Add your mixture to paper cake cases so that the mixture comes to about halfway up each case. This will mean your cakes will have room to rise once they start to bake.

5. Place in the oven and bake for 15 minutes, until they are a lovely golden brown colour.

6. While they're in the oven, mix together the butter and icing sugar for your topping.

7. When the cakes are out of the oven, leave them to cool. Then very carefully cut a small circle from the very top of each cake. Cut each circle in half – these are your butterfly wings!

8. In the space left where you've cut a piece away from each cake, place a blob of yummy topping. Then carefully place the two wings on top, so that the topping holds them in place. Perfect!

Visit the Website!

There's a whole Jacqueline Wilson town to explore! You can generate your own special username, customise your online bedroom, test your knowledge of Jacqueline's books with fun quizzes and puzzles, and upload book reviews. There's lots of fun stuff to discover, including competitions, book trailers, and Jacqueline's scrapbook. And if you love writing, visit the special storytelling area!

Plus, you can hear the latest news from Jacqueline in her monthly diary, find out whether she's doing events near you, read her fan-mail replies, and chat to other fans on the message boards!

www.jacquelinewilson.co.uk

HAVE YOU READ JACQUELINE'S 100TH BOOK?

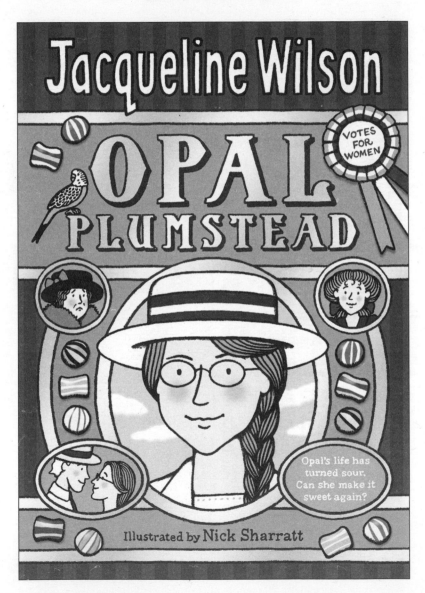

Jacqueline Wilson

OPAL PLUMSTEAD

VOTES FOR WOMEN

Opal's life has turned sour. Can she make it sweet again?

Illustrated by Nick Sharratt

THE HETTY FEATHER ADVENTURES!